James Hadley Chase and The Murder Room

>>> This title is part of The Murder Room, our series dedicated to making available out-of-print or hard-to-find titles by classic crime writers.

Crime fiction has always held up a mirror to society. The Victorians were fascinated by sensational murder and the emerging science of detection; now we are obsessed with the forensic detail of violent death. And no other genre has so captivated and enthralled readers.

Vast troves of classic crime writing have for a long time been unavailable to all but the most dedicated frequenters of second-hand bookshops. The advent of digital publishing means that we are now able to bring you the backlists of a huge range of titles by classic and contemporary crime writers, some of which have been out of print for decades.

From the genteel amateur private eyes of the Golden Age and the femmes fatales of pulp fiction, to the morally ambiguous hard-boiled detectives of mid twentieth-century America and their descendants who walk our twenty-first century streets, The Murder Room has it all. **>>>**

The Murder Room
Where Criminal Minds Meet

themurderroom.com

T0352489

James Hadley Chase (1906–1985)

Born René Brabazon Raymond in London, the son of a British colonel in the Indian Army, James Hadley Chase was educated at King's School in Rochester, Kent, and left home at the age of 18. He initially worked in book sales until, inspired by the rise of gangster culture during the Depression and by reading James M. Cain's *The Postman Always Rings Twice*, he wrote his first novel, *No Orchids for Miss Blandish*. Despite the American setting of many of his novels, Chase (like Peter Cheyney, another hugely successful British noir writer) never lived there, writing with the aid of maps and a slang dictionary. He had phenomenal success with the novel, which continued unabated throughout his entire career, spanning 45 years and nearly 90 novels. His work was published in dozens of languages and over thirty titles were adapted for film. He served in the RAF during World War II, where he also edited the RAF Journal. In 1956 he moved to France with his wife and son; they later moved to Switzerland, where Chase lived until his death in 1985.

By James Hadley Chase
(published in The Murder Room)

Want to Stay Alive?

James Hadley Chase

An Orion book

Copyright © Hervey Raymond 1972

The right of James Hadley Chase to be identified as the author of this
work has been asserted in accordance with the Copyright, Designs and
Patents Act 1988.

This edition published by
The Orion Publishing Group Ltd
Orion House
5 Upper St Martin's Lane
London WC2H 9EA

An Hachette UK company
A CIP catalogue record for this book is available from the British Library

ISBN 978 1 4719 0374 8

www.orionbooks.co.uk

One

They hadn't been asleep for more than an hour when Meg woke with a start. She lifted her head from the rucksack that served as a pillow and peered uneasily around the unfurnished moon-lit room. Cobwebs hung in thick festoons and a giant spider moved across the ceiling.

'A spooky place,' she had said to Chuck when they had bro-ken in. 'A place for ghosts.'

But Chuck had no imagination. He had sneered at her.

'Okay ... so we keep them company. Anything's better than these mosquitoes.'

They had come on the derelict house as they had left High-way 4 to look for somewhere to sleep. Their money had run out soon after leaving Goulds, a citron and potato town. Chuck had tried to get a job at one of the packing plants but they had turned him away. His shoulder-length hair, his beard and his smell that had built up on him since leaving Jacksonville where he had had his last wash made him a non-starter.

This deserted house stood in a jungle of stunted palms, palm-ettoes and flowering shrubs. It was a Southern colonial two storey building with six square porch columns reaching to the roof: a rich man's house that must have been impressive in its day.

Meg had stared curiously at the building and had wondered who the owner had been and why no one wanted to buy it.

'Who cares?' Chuck had said when she had expressed her thoughts and going up to the entrance doors, he had aimed a kick at the heavy iron lock. The doors sagged open. One of them came away from its hinges and fell with a clatter, raising chok-ing dust.

Meg had drawn back.

'I don't want to sleep in there . . . it's spooky.'

'Oh, shut up!' Chuck was in no mood to listen to her talk. He was hungry, tired and depressed. He caught hold of her arm and pulled her into the dusty darkness.

They decided to sleep on the upper floor as the lower win-dows were boarded up. The moonlight, coming through the dirty window panes up there was strong enough for them to see to unpack. The wide staircase was impressive. Meg imagined

1

someone like Scarlet O'Hara descending the stairs in all her finery, watched by a group of admirers, waiting for her in the big hall. She didn't pass this thought on to Chuck. She knew he would only jeer at her. Chuck lived essentially in the present. Even the future was a blank wall to him.

Now, suddenly awake, her heart beginning to beat unevenly, she listened.

The house seemed alive. The wind coming off Biscayne Bay moaned softly in the eaves. The shredding wallpaper made soft rattling noises. The woodwork creaked, and somewhere below a door swung in the wind, its rusty hinges squeaking.

Meg listened for some moments, then reluctantly settled to sleep again. She looked over at Chuck who lay on his back. his mouth half open, a strand of his long, dirty hair lying across his face. Even from where she lay she could smell him, but that didn't bother her. She probably smelt herself. They would fix that up when they reached the sea and could have a bathe.

She looked up at the ceiling, spreading her long legs and cupping her full breasts, covered by a thin, dirty sweater.

By now she had got used to living rough. It had many advantages: at least she was free to go where she liked and to live how she liked, and this was important to her.

She thought of her father working for peanuts as an insurance salesman and her dreary mother. Until she was seventeen years of age she had gone along with them, but even at the age of fourteen, she had made up her mind that the moment she was sure enough of herself to quit, she would quit. This middle-class, suffocating life was not for her. It wasn't until Chuck met her that she had made the break.

Chuck was four years older than she. She had been to a movie on her own: something she seldom did for she always had lots of friends. This particular night she wanted to be alone. She had told her parents she was meeting Shirly and they were going to a movie down town. She always had to tell her parents who she was meeting and she always lied, knowing they were too dumb to check. She lied even when she went with Shirly, telling them she was going with Edna. She got a kick out of lying to her parents. She wondered if they even heard what she told them. Often she wondered if they would say anything different from the usual 'have a good time, honey, and don't be late' while they stared at the TV screen if she said she was going out with Frank Sinatra.

The movie turned out to be a drag and she left half way through it. As soon as she got into the hot night air and realised it was only 21.00 she regretted leaving the movie house. She now had nothing to do except go home, and the thought of watching TV with her parents filled her with dismay.

'Are you looking for company?'

Chuck had moved out of the shadows and stood before her. She regarded him appraisingly. Meg had done everything a teenager will do with men except surrender her virginity. She liked the struggles in cars when she kept her legs tightly crossed and submitted to everything except that one thing. She had been warned so often by her mother to have nothing to do with strangers that the warning was now a bore and a challenge.

Chuck had a certain appeal. He was short, stocky and powerfully built. His long reddish hair and beard pleased her. His face was attractive in its care-free ugliness. He had a virility that stirred her.

She recalled how they had gone down to the beach and had swum naked. Chuck was so natural about his nakedness that he killed any shyness that Meg had to strip off.

When they reached the sea, he had said, 'Let's swim.' He had taken off his clothes before Meg realised what was happening and naked, he had run into the sea. After a moment's hesitation, she had followed his example and later had submitted to his urgency.

Her first sexual experience had been explosive. Although Chuck had many failings, he knew how to handle a woman.

'I like you, Meg,' he had said as they lay side by side, drained and relaxed. 'Have you any money?'

She was to learn that money and sex were the only two things in which Chuck was interested. She had saved three hundred dollars from presents given her from wealthy relations over the years, saved against a 'rainy day' as her mother had put it. This wasn't a rainy day, but why should she care?

Chuck told her he planned to go to Florida. He wanted the sun. No, he didn't do anything. When he ran out of money, he got a job – any job – and when he had saved enough, he quit. It was a good way to live and Meg thought so too. With three hundred dollars they could live forever, Chuck had said. How about going with him?

This was the moment Meg had been waiting for. She had found an exciting man whose thinking was the same as hers.

3

He was strong, tough, reckless and his love making terrific. She didn't hesitate.

They arranged to meet at the Greyhound bus station the following day and they would go together to Florida.

The following morning, when her mother was out shopping, she had packed her camping outfit, written a note to say she wasn't coming back, helped herself to fifty dollars her father kept in the house also for a rainy day and left home for good.

Her three hundred dollars and her father's fifty dollars didn't last forever as Chuck had predicted. Among his many weaknesses was a compulsive urge to gamble. Meg sat with a hammering heart as Chuck cheerfully rolled dice with two youths who they had picked up on their way down to Jacksonville. When Chuck was down to their last fifty dollars, Meg had said in a trembling voice that it was time to stop.

The two youths had looked at Chuck. The elder had said, 'Do you take that kind of crap from your woman?'

Chuck had put his broad, short fingered hand over Meg's face and had given her a shove that sent her flying to land on the uneven ground with a jar that shook the breath out of her. By the time she had recovered, Chuck had lost the rest of their money and the two youths had faded away into the darkness.

'So what's money for?' Chuck had snarled at her when she had screamed at him. 'Shut up! We'll get more ... there's always money!'

They had got jobs as orange pickers and had toiled in the heat for a week until they had scraped together thirty dollars, then they quit and started once more towards Miami.

The money didn't last long after paying the fares and buying food. Now they had nothing and Meg was hungry. They hadn't eaten for twelve hours: the last meal had been a greasy hamburger, and yet she still had no regrets. This kind of life: being dirty, hungry, homeless was a lot better than living in that dreary prison ruled by her parents.

Well, something will turn up tomorrow, she thought. She had faith in Chuck. She again settled herself to sleep, then again she started up.

Someone was moving around in the hall below!

She distinctly heard the scrape of shoe leather and her heart began to race. She shifted silently over to Chuck and taking hold of his arm, she gently shook it.

'Chuck!'

4

He moaned, threw off her hand and began to turn over, but she shook his arm again.

'Chuck!'

'Oh, for God's sake!' He came awake and half sat up. His smell of dirt even at this moment made her wrinkle her nose. 'What's the matter?'

'There's someone moving around downstairs.'

As she gripped his arm, she felt his steel muscles tighten and she was reassured. His physical strength made a tremendous impression on her.

'Listen!' she whispered.

He shook off her hand and got to his feet. Moving silently, he went to the door and gently opened it. She looked at his broad back. His crouch and steadiness helped to diminish her fear. He listened for a long moment, then shut the door and came over to her.

'Yeah ... you're right. There is someone down there ... could be a cop.'

She stared at him.

'A cop?'

'We're trespassing. If some nosey cop ...' He chewed on his lower lip. 'We could get knocked off for vagrancy.'

'We're not doing any harm ... vagrancy?'

Chuck wasn't listening. He took an object from his hip pocket and pushed it into Meg's hand.

'Put it down your pants. If it's a cop he mustn't find it on me.'

'What is it?'

'A knife, stupid!' He went to the door and opened it softly. Meg watched him walk out and pause at the head of the stairs. She stared at the bone handle of the knife with its chrome button and her finger touched the button. She flinched as three inches of gleaming steel snapped into sight. She had no idea how to return the blade into the handle and getting to her feet, she crossed the room and hid the knife under a pile of mildewing shreds of wallpaper. Then she joined Chuck. He waved her to be silent. They both stood motionless, listening. All Meg could hear was the rapid beating of her heart.

'I'm going down,' Chuck whispered.

She caught hold of his arm.

'No!'

He didn't seem to need any further persuasion. She had the

idea he was as scared as she was and she was faintly disappointed in him. They stood there listening for several more moments, then they heard someone walking in the room to the left of the hall. Then a shadowy figure came into the hall. They could see the red glow of a cigarette and Chuck relaxed. He was sure whoever the intruder was, he wasn't a cop. Cops don't smoke on duty.

'Who's that?' he demanded, and to Meg his voice sounded harsh and tough.

There was a moment's pause. They could see the shadowy figure standing motionless, then the beam of a powerful flashlight hit them, making them start back. The beam remained on them for a second or so, then it went out, leaving them blind.

'Get me the knife,' Chuck whispered.

Meg stumbled into the room, ran over to the heap of wallpaper and found the knife.

'I saw the door was open,' a man was saying from below as she joined Chuck, 'so I walked in.'

Chuck's hot, sweaty fingers closed around the handle of the knife.

'Then walk out again,' he snarled. 'We have first claim. Scram!'

'It's big enough for all of us, isn't it? I have food. I don't like eating alone.'

Meg heard her stomach rumble. The thought of eating made saliva fill her mouth. She gripped Chuck's arm. He got the message. He was starving too.

'I thought you were a cop,' he said. 'Come on up.'

They watched the man below move into the room off the hall and return, carrying a rucksack. He started up the stairs, using his flashlight.

Keeping his knife in his hand, Chuck waited for him, pushing Meg back towards the room they had just left. She paused in the doorway, her heart beating uneasily as the man reached the head of the stairs.

Chuck peered at him. All he could see was a tall outline: a man a head taller than himself, but slimly built and without his shoulder spread. Not much strength, Chuck decided and relaxed a little.

'Let's have a look at you,' Chuck said in his bullying voice. 'Give me your flash.'

6

The man offered the flashlight. Taking it, Chuck swung the beam on the man's face.

Watching, Meg stiffened. This man was a Seminole Indian. She had seen several such Indians on the way down from Jacksonville, and she recognised the thick blue-black hair, the dark skin, the high cheekbones and the narrow black eyes. This man was around twenty-three or four and handsome, but his wooden, expressionless face and his stillness made her uneasy. He wore a yellow pattern shirt, dotted with white flowers, dark blue hipsters and his brown feet were thrust into rope soled slippers.

He stood still, letting them both examine him. In the light of the flashlight, his eyes seemed to Meg to be on fire.

'Who are you?' Chuck demanded, lowering the beam to the floor.

'Poke Toholo is my name,' the man said. 'And you?'

'I'm Chuck Rogers . . . this is my girl, Meg.'

'Let's eat.'

Lighting the way, Chuck led the way into the room. Meg had already gone ahead and was sitting by her rucksack, her stomach was cringing with emptiness.

Poke dumped his rucksack on the floor, knelt, opened it and produced two candles which he lit, then stuck them to the floor. He reached up and took the flashlight from Chuck and put it in the rucksack, then he produced a roast chicken and several slices of ham from a plastic sack.

'Hey! Where did you get this from?' Chuck said, his eyes growing round. He couldn't remember when he had eaten chicken last.

Poke looked at him.

'Should you care?' He divided the chicken into equal parts skilfully, using a bone-handled knife.

They ate in silence, savagely and contentedly. Meg noticed the Indian kept looking at Chuck, then away. He didn't once look at her.

When they had finished, Chuck rested back on his elbows.

'Man! That was good! Where are you heading for?'

Poke produced a pack of cigarettes.

'Paradise City. And you?'

'Miami, I guess.'

They lit their cigarettes from a candle flame.

7

'Have you a job to go to?' Poke asked. He was sitting crossed legged, his hands on his knees.

'I'll find one.'

'Think so?' Poke stared at Chuck. 'Cops don't dig for bums.'

Chuck stiffened.

'You calling me a bum?'

'What else are you? You're dirty and you stink.'

Meg flinched. She was sure Chuck would attack this Indian with his knife and she was startled when Chuck remained where he was.

'I'd rather be a bum than a buck savage,' he said. 'You think you'll get a job?'

'I don't need a job.'

Chuck stiffened to attention.

'You got money then?'

Poke nodded.

'How much? Ten bucks? I bet you haven't that!'

'I'm buying a car tomorrow.'

Chuck's breath hissed between his teeth.

'A car? What kind of a car?'

Poke shrugged.

'Something cheap . . . second hand. I need a car.'

'For Pete's sake!' Chuck stared at the Indian for a long moment. 'Hey! Why don't we three gang up? Suppose we come with you as far as Paradise City . . . what do you say?'

Listening, Meg marvelled at Chuck's nerve. He was right, of course. If you didn't ask, you didn't get.

'Why should we join up?' Poke asked after a pause.

'What have you got to lose? No fun in travelling alone. We'll keep you company.'

Poke got to his feet and carrying his rucksack to the far end of the room, away from the other two, he sat down.

'You deaf?' Chuck said. 'What have you got to lose?'

'I'll think about it. I'm going to sleep. Blow the candles out . . . they cost money.' and Poke stretched out on the floor.

Chuck and Meg exchanged glances as they watched the Indian turn over on his side, his back to them, his head on his rucksack.

Meg leaned forward and blew out the candles. Darkness closed in on them. It was several minutes before their eyes grew accustomed to the moonlight. By that time, Poke seemed to be sleeping. His breathing was slow and steady.

Chuck and Meg settled down.

Her hunger satisfied, her body tired, Meg slid into sleep, but not Chuck. He lay still, his mind active.

Was this Indian bluffing? he asked himself. Could he really be planning to buy a car? If he meant what he said he must have the money either on him or in his rucksack.

Chuck began to sweat. He must have at least two hundred dollars! A goddam Redskin with two hundred dollars!

His thick, short fingers closed around the handle of his knife. It would be easy. He had only to creep across the room and one slash with the knife would finish it.

Chuck was no stranger to murder. It was always the first one that counted and he had two behind him. What was one more?

Then he remembered Meg and he grimaced. He should never have picked her up. He was sure she wouldn't stand for him killing the Indian. His fingers tightened their grip on his knife. Two hundred dollars! Well, if she didn't go along, then she would have to go the same way. He would be miles from here before the bodies were found – if they were ever found.

He wiped his sweating face with the back of his hand.

Yes, he would do it! But not yet. The Indian was sleeping lightly. Later, the light sleep would turn heavy . . . that would be the time.

'Chuck?'

The sound of the Indian's voice made Chuck stiffen.

'I sleep light and I have a gun.' There was a pause, then Poke went on, 'We'll talk tomorrow.'

A gun!

Chuck's fingers relaxed on the handle of the knife. It was as if this bastard had read his thoughts.

'Oh, shut up,' he growled. 'I'm trying to sleep.'

'We'll talk tomorrow.'

Eventually, Chuck did fall asleep.

*

For breakfast Poke supplied more ham, some stale bread and a bottle of coke.

They ate in silence, but again Meg was aware that Poke kept looking at Chuck, his black eyes glittering as if he were trying to make up his mind about him.

When they had finished, Chuck said abruptly, 'When you buy that car, are you giving us a ride?'

9

Poke went over to his rucksack and produced a cordless electric razor and a pocket mirror. Propping the mirror against the window frame, he began to shave.

Chuck clenched his fists and blood rushed into his face.

'Did you hear what I said?' he snarled.

Poke glanced at him, then went on shaving. When he had finished, he said, 'I'm still thinking.' He cleaned the razor and put it away, then took out a towel and a piece of soap. 'The canal is just across the way. You coming?'

Chuck's heart skipped a beat. Here was his chance! Away from Meg! He could kill this Indian, come back, and tell her he had drowned. She mightn't believe it, but at least she wouldn't be a witness.

'Sure.'

He followed Poke out of the room. At the foot of the stairs, he said, 'Hell! I've forgotten my towel.'

His brown face wooden, Poke stared at him.

'Tell her not to bother. I have the money on me,' and he crossed the hall and walked out into the sunlight.

Chuck returned to the room, his face red with fury. He found a filthy towel in his rucksack as Meg said, 'Do you think he'll let us go with him?'

'How the hell do I know?' Chuck snarled and left the room.

He caught up with Poke who led the way through the undergrowth to the canal.

Chuck thought: I'll take him when we've stripped off. I don't want any blood on me: a knee in the groin, then the knife.

They reached the canal. The water sparkled in the sunlight. On the far side, Chuck could see Highway 27 that led to Miami. At this early hour there was no passing traffic.

He pulled off his grimy shirt and flexed his muscles. Poke wandered away from him. He took off his clothes and moved to the edge of the canal.

Looking at him, Chuck saw he was wearing a plastic money-belt around his slim waist. The belt looked bulky and Chuck's eyes narrowed, then he felt sudden apprehension as his eyes moved over Poke's body. He had never seen such a build. Flat muscles rippled with every movement. This was a body that seemed to be made of flexible steel and Chuck suddenly lost confidence in his own strength. Maybe this Indian wouldn't be so easy to take. His hand went to his hip pocket and his fingers closed on the handle of his knife.

He watched Poke dive into the canal and begin to swim with powerful strokes towards the far side. Turning his back, Chuck took from his pocket a thick elastic band which he slipped onto his wrist. He fastened the knife to his wrist by sliding it under the band. Then taking off his trousers and kicking off his shoes, he dived into the water. He was a clumsy swimmer and not at home in the water. He saw Poke had turned on his back and was floating. He heaved himself through the water towards him. A powerful stab upwards would finish the job, but he had to get that belt off before he let the body sink.

He was now within a few yards of Poke. He trod water.

'Pretty good, huh?' he said, his voice husky.

Poke nodded.

Chuck made a stroke to bring himself closer. The gap between the two men closed, then suddenly Poke sank out of sight. Where he had just been was now a ripple of water.

Cursing to himself, Chuck waited, his eyes searching the surface of the canal. He felt steel like fingers grip his ankles and he was dragged down, water filling his mouth and nostrils. He kicked out wildly, thrashing around, felt the grip slacken and the fingers leave his ankles. He came to the surface, spluttering and gasping. When he had shaken the water out of his eyes, he saw Poke swimming away from him. The knife that had been strapped to his wrist was gone!

Chuck started for the bank, frustrated rage swamping caution, but Poke easily beat him to it. He was already on the bank as Chuck scrambled out of the water.

With a bellow of rage, Chuck went for the Indian like a charging bull, his head down, his thick fingers hooked and groping. Poke weaved aside and as Chuck blundered by him, he kicked Chuck's legs from under him, bringing him down with a body shattering thud.

Then Poke was on him. His knee slammed into his chest and Chuck saw his own knife in the Indian's hand. The razor sharp, glittering blade touched Chuck's throat.

Chuck cringed. He looked into the glittering black eyes and with terror he thought his life was about to be wiped out.

Poke regarded him, the point of the knife pricking Chuck's skin.

'You were going to kill me?' he asked softly. 'Don't lie! Tell me!'

'I wanted the money,' Chuck gasped.

11

'You want money badly enough to kill?'

They looked at each other, then Poke stood up and moved back. Chuck struggled to his feet. He was shaking and sweat ran from his face.

'You want my money?' Poke said. 'You're welcome to it if you can get it.' He tapped the plastic belt. 'Two hundred and twenty dollars.' He looked at the knife, then holding it by the blade, he offered the handle to Chuck. 'Take it.'

Bewildered, Chuck snatched at the knife. Poke watched him.

'Take my money if you can.'

Chuck looked at the Indian. The glittering eyes and his stillness like a snake waiting to strike frightened him. His nerve failed. The knife slid out of his fingers and dropped onto the grass.

'So you're not stupid,' Poke said. 'Go and wash. You smell.'

Cowed, Chuck took the piece of soap Poke was now offering him and went down the bank into the water. When he had washed and dried himself, Poke was dressed and sitting on the bank, smoking a cigarette. He watched Chuck get into his dirty clothes, then beckoned to him.

Like a hypnotised rabbit, Chuck came and sat by his side.

'I've been looking for a man like you,' Poke said. 'A man without a conscience. You would have killed me for two hundred and twenty dollars ... how many people would you kill for two thousand dollars?'

Chuck licked his lips. This Indian was out of his head. He thought of the moment when the knife could have slit his throat and he shivered.

'You live like a neglected pig,' Poke went on. 'You are dirty, you are hungry, you stink. Look at me! When I want something I take it. I shave because I stole a razor. I stole the chicken and the ham from a Self Service store. I stole this money.' He tapped his waist. 'Two hundred and twenty dollars! Do you know how I stole all that money? It was easy. A man gave me a ride and I threatened him. I have a gun. When people are frightened they pay up. All I had to do was to show him the gun and he gave me the money. It's very simple. Fear is the key that unlocks the wallets and handbags of the rich.' He turned to stare at Chuck. 'I have the formula for fear.'

Chuck didn't understand. All he knew was he wanted to get away from this Indian. He was sure he was crazy.

12

Poke took a pack of cigarettes from his shirt pocket and offered it. After hesitating, Chuck took one and lit up.

'Tell me about yourself,' Poke said. 'I don't want lies. I think I can use you. Tell me about yourself.'

'Use me? What do you mean?'

Chuck had a creepy feeling this Indian wasn't bluffing. Two thousand dollars!

"How do I do that?"

'Tell me about yourself.'

Confident he had nothing to lose, Chuck talked.

He admitted he was semi-illiterate. He could read, but wrote with difficulty. His mother was a prostitute. He never knew his father. At the age of eight, he was a leader of a gang of kids who stole from stores. Later, he acted as his mother's pimp. He was continually being chased by the cops and at the age of eighteen he had killed a cop. This cop had been the most hated man on the block and finally Chuck had ambushed him and had battered him to death with an iron bar. At twenty, he had come up against another youth who imagined he could take over Chuck's mob. There had been a knife fight and Chuck had won. His opponent's body had been fed into a cement mixer and his bones and flesh had gone into the foundations of a new slum tenement. His mother had met a violent end. Chuck had found her with her throat slit. She had left him a hundred dollars and he had cleared out of the district and taken to the road. He had been on the road for the past year, picking up a living here and there, living rough and not giving a damn about anything.

He tossed his cigarette butt into the canal.

'That's the photo. What's this you said about two thousand dollars?'

'So you've killed two men.' Poke stared at him. 'If you join up with me there will be other killings. That bother you?'

'I don't want to stick my neck out,' Chuck said after a long moment. 'Tell me about the money.'

'That will be your cut.'

Chuck drew in a deep breath.

'What's the racket then?'

'Something I have been planning for months: an idea that will work, but I can't handle it alone. Tell me about this girl you have with you. I could use her too.'

'Meg?' Chuck shrugged. 'She ran off from home. She's a good screw. I don't know anything else about her.'

'I could use her.'

Chuck's little eyes narrowed as he thought. Then reluctantly, he shook his head.

'She wouldn't dig for killing.'

'I want a girl. It's part of the plan. Could you sell her the idea?'

'How the hell do I know? I don't know what you're talking about! What's this racket?'

Poke stared at him. The glittering black eyes continued to worry Chuck.

'Are you sure you want to know?'

'What do you mean? Of course I want to know!'

'You said just now you didn't want to stick your neck out.'

'For two thousand dollars, I'll stick my neck out. What is it?'

Poke continued to stare at him.

'If I tell you and you change your mind and don't want to go along, you won't leave here alive. This is something I've been planning for some time. Once I've told you, it won't be my secret, will it? You're either in or you're dead.'

Chuck saw there was a blunt nosed gun in the Indian's hand. It had appeared like a conjuring trick. He flinched back. Guns scared him.

'Make up your mind.' Poke stared down at the gun. 'If you want out, get up and go and I'll find someone else. If you want in, you'd better not change your mind.'

'What'll it be worth to me?' Chuck said to gain time.

'I told you . . . two thousand dollars.'

'And these killings . . . how safe will they be?'

'There will be three . . . they will be safe. I've got it planned. I don't stick my neck out even though my cut will be bigger than yours.'

Two thousand dollars! Chuck thought what he could do with all that money.

'I'm in . . . go ahead and tell me,' he said.

Poke put the gun back in his hip pocket.

'And the girl?'

'Leave her to me. I'll talk her into it.'

'Fear is the key that opens wallets and handbags,' Poke said. 'I have found a formula for fear.'

Looking at the expressionless brown face, the glittering black eyes and the Indian's unnatural stillness, Chuck suddenly had the urge to stop him telling him more. Then he again thought of the money.

A trickle of sweat ran down his forehead, down the bridge of his nose and dripped into his chin.

He listened as the Indian talked and as he listened he realised the Indian was on to a soft touch.

'We need a target rifle,' Poke concluded. 'There's a gunsmith in Paradise City. It'll be easy. When we have it, we're in business.'

'You know the City?' Chuck asked.

A strange, bitter smile crossed Poke's lips.

'Yes. One time it was where I lived. Yes, I know it.'

Chuck was curious. He had told this Indian about himself. He felt entitled to be told in return.

'Did you work there?'

Poke got to his feet.

'I'm now going to buy the car.' He stared Chuck. 'You're in?'

Chuck nodded.

'I'm in.'

'Talk to the girl. If you're not sure of her, we leave her. We can find some other girl.'

'Okay.'

Chuck watched Poke walk away towards the highway, then picking up his towel, he went uneasily back to the derelict house.

*

It was after Meg had bathed in the canal and was drying her hair that Chuck came to sit with her on the bank.

Half an hour ago, she had been waiting anxiously for him and had asked immediately if Poke was going to take them with him in the car.

'Have a wash,' Chuck had said. 'We'll talk later.'

Now as he sat down beside her, she repeated the question.

'Are we going with him?'

'I am,' Chuck said, not looking at her.

Meg dropped the towel. She felt a clutch of fear that turned her cold.

'You are? What about me?'

Chuck plucked a handful of grass and tossed it into the air.

'Maybe from now on you'll be better off on your own.'

'What do you mean?' Meg got up on her knees. 'You're not walking out on me?'

Seeing the panic in her eyes, he hid a grin. He lay back, resting his head on his hands as he stared up at the blue sky.

'Look, baby, I'm sick of living this way. I want money.' He took a crumpled pack of cigarettes from his shirt pocket. 'You want one?'

'Chuck! You're not aiming to leave me?'

He lit the cigarette, taking his time.

'Just listen, will you? To get real money, you have to take risks,' he said finally as she knelt at his side, watching him fearfully. 'I don't want you to get involved, so maybe it'd be better if you and me parted.'

Meg closed her eyes.

'You mean you don't want me any more ... you're sick of me?'

'I didn't say that, did I?' Chuck drew in smoke and let it drift down his nostrils. 'Can't you listen? I'm thinking of you. I like you so why get you mixed up in something dangerous? I don't want to lose you, but I'm pretty sure you wouldn't have the nerve to go through with this so we'd better part.'

'This? What do you mean ... this?' Meg's voice became shrill.

'Poke's onto a smart racket. He needs me and he also needs a girl.' Chuck was pleased with the way he was handling this. 'It could get rough. It could land you behind bars for twenty years.'

Meg turned cold. So they were planning something criminal! She had been with Chuck now for two months and although he had often talked of stealing, he had never done it. She had had the idea if she had encouraged him he would have done it, but she had always begged him not to do it in spite of them both being hungry at times. She realised this Indian had influenced Chuck. By his talk, he was pushing Chuck over the edge.

'Chuck!' She caught hold of his hand. 'Let's go! Let's leave before he comes back! He's sick in the head. I know he is. We'll get a job somewhere together. We've managed fine so far. I'll work for you ... I ...'

'Oh, shut up!' Chuck snarled. 'I'm joining him so don't start that sob stuff! *You* go and get a job ... if that's the way you like it. Do you want to stay out in the sun picking goddam oranges for the rest of your life – If you do ... go ahead!'

Meg saw it was hopeless to persuade him. She drew in a shuddering breath of despair. An orange picker? What else unless she went home! She thought of her parents, three meals a day, routine, getting up, going to her father's office, typing, going to bed, getting up, going to the office.

'Would you get twenty years too?' she asked.

Chuck crushed out his cigarette.

'Oh, sure, if it turned sour which it won't, but I don't give a damn. I want quick money and this will be quick money! Poke says he'll pay you five hundred to do this job. He thinks you'll do it, but I said you wouldn't. I said it wasn't your style.' He scratched his beard. 'I said you hadn't the guts.'

The money meant nothing to Meg, but being left on her own did. After two months with Chuck, she couldn't imagine life without him.

'What will I have to do?'

Chuck turned his head so she shouldn't see his smirk of triumph.

'What you're told. Look, baby, the less you know about this the safer for you and for me. You can come along with us if and only if you do what Poke tells you without asking questions and without arguing. You get five hundred. When it's finished you and me can go off to Los Angeles.'

'But, Chuck, this isn't fair! Can't you see that? I don't know what I'm walking into!' Meg beat her clenched fists onto her knees. 'You say I could go to prison for twenty years and you won't tell me . . . it's not fair!'

'Oh, sure, but that's the proposition.' Chuck got to his feet. 'Take it or leave it, baby. Think it over. Poke and I leave in about half an hour. It's up to you if you come with us.'

He was sure now he had her on the hook.

As he moved away, she said, 'Chuck . . .'

'What is it?'

'Do you trust him?'

'I don't trust anyone, including you,' Chuck said. 'I never have, but I do know he's on to a soft touch. I do know he and I are going to make some fast money and that's all I care about. You have half an hour.' He stared at her. 'And remember, baby, once you're in, you stay in . . . there's no out . . . understand?' and he walked away.

Meg sat for a long time staring at the glittering water of the canal. Poke frightened her. She knew he was evil and a little mad. She knew she would lose Chuck if she said no. After all, she told herself finally, if things got too rough she could end her life. Her life was the only thing she really owned. The only thing that really and truly belonged to her. Enough pills, a razor blade across her wrists and it would be finished ... anything was better than to be left here without Chuck and without money and on her own.

She got to her feet and started back to the derelict house. Chuck had packed his rucksack and was sitting on the top step, a cigarette dangling between his lips. He looked at her, the smoke making his little eyes squint.

'I'll pack,' she said. 'I'm coming with you.'

'You're going to do what you're told ... no questions?'

She nodded.

Chuck's grin was suddenly warm and friendly.

'Fine. You know something?'

'What?'

'I wouldn't want to have lost you.'

Meg felt tears rush to her eyes. This was the nicest thing anyone had ever said to her. The way her thin, white face lit up told Chuck he had said absolutely the right thing. He got up and she ran into his arms. He cupped her small buttocks and pulled her hard against him.

'Oh, Chuck ... will it work out?' He could feel her trembling. 'I'm scared. That Indian ... he's crazy ... I'm sure he is.'

'You leave him to me, baby. Go and get packed.'

Twenty minutes later, Poke Toholo pulled up in front of them in an old Buick convertible. Although a little battered, its chrome work gleamed. It was an anonymous car: dark blue with a dark blue top and faded red leather seats: a car you wouldn't notice among the thousands of cars that rolled along Highway 4.

Seeing Chuck and Meg sitting on the steps, their rucksacks packed told him Chuck had played his cards right. He got out of the car and joined them.

'Okay?' he said, looking at Meg.

She nodded, feeling herself shrink inside as she met the black, glittering eyes.

He turned to Chuck.

'Our first stop will be Fulford. You'll get rid of that beard and get your hair cut. When we reach Paradise City we're all going to look like three respectable people on vacation. You've got to get your clothes washed.'

Chuck grimaced. He was proud of his long hair and beard.

'Okay,' he said, shrugging. 'Anything you say.'

Picking up the two rucksacks, he went with Poke to the car.

For a long moment, Meg sat there, feeling the sun on her face, then as Poke started the engine, she lifted her shoulders in a resigned shrug and joined them.

Two

Detective 1st Grade Tom Lepski stroke into the Detectives' room at Paradise City's Police Headquarters like a man ten feet tall. His promotion from 2nd Grade had come through the previous day: a promotion he had been sweating for for the past eighteen months. The news had come in time for him to arrange a celebration. He had bought Carroll, his wife, an orchid, taken her to an expensive restaurant, got a little drunk and completed the evening to his satisfaction: Carroll had put out her best performance since their honeymoon night.

Lepski, tall, lean with steely blue eyes was an ambitious, shrewd cop whose opinion of himself was slightly higher than his actual achievements.

Sergeant Joe Beigler, the doyen of the Detectives' desk, was catching the early morning stint. He leaned back in his chair when he saw Lepski and said with heavy sarcasm, 'Now, the City's safe. Take the chair, Tom. I'll go feed my face.'

Always oblivious of sarcasm, Lepski shot his cuffs and moved to Beigler's desk.

'Relax, Sarg. I'll handle anything that comes up. Any news of Fred?'

Sergeant Fred Hess, Homicide division, was in hospital with a broken leg. If he hadn't been the main stay of the division, the breaking of his leg would have been one of the big laughs at headquarters. Hess had a six-year-old son, Fred Hess junior, known in the district as the Monster of Mulberry Avenue where Hess lived. The kid had tossed a kitten, owned by a sour old spinster, up a tree just for the hell of it. Hess, rather than face the spinster and feeling responsible, had climbed the tree to rescue the kitten, watched by admiring neighbours. A bough had broken and Hess had descended to the ground with some violence, breaking his leg. The kitten, of course, had come down on its own steam and Fred Hess junior had stood over his groaning father, grinning his death's head grin, asking what the fuss was all about. It was only by fleetness of foot that saved him from a clip on the ear, thrown at him by his infuriated father.

'Fred?' Beigler grinned. 'He's disgracing himself. The nurses are complaining about his language, but he's mending. He should be up and out in a couple of weeks.'

'I'll call him,' Lepski said. 'I don't want him to worry. If he knows I'm handling his job, he'll relax.'

Beigler looked alarmed.

'Don't do that. We want him back quick. A call like that could harden his arteries.'

As Beigler left, Lepski looked over at Detective 2nd Grade Max Jacoby who was hiding a grin.

'Did you hear that?' he demanded. 'Do you think Joe's jealous of me?'

'Who isn't, Tom? Even I envy you.'

'You do?' Lepski was pleased. 'Yeah ...' He shrugged. 'Well, that's the way it goes. I guess I must learn to live with it. Anything cooking?'

'Not a thing. The blotter's clean.'

Lepski settled himself more comfortably in his chair.

'What I want now is a nice juicy murder ... a sex killing. While Fred is out of the way, this could be my big chance.' He lit a cigarette and stared off into space. 'I know Fred's no fool, but that goes for me too. Now I've got my promotion, Carroll's already nagging me to try for Sergeant. Women are never satisfied.' He sighed, shaking his head. 'You're lucky not to be married.'

'Don't I know it,' Jacoby said with feeling. 'Me for freedom!'

Lepski scowled at him.

'Don't think I'm knocking marriage. There's a lot to be said for it. A young guy like you should get married. You ...'

The telephone bell interrupted him.

'See?' Lepski smirked. 'The moment I walk in, there's action.' He scooped up the receiver. 'Police headquarters. Detective 1st Grade Lepski talking.'

Jacoby hid a grin.

'Give me Sergeant Beigler,' a male voice barked.

'Sergeant Beigler is off duty,' Lepski said, frowning. Who was this jerk who thought Beigler a better contact than himself? 'What is it?'

'This is Hartley Danvaz. Is Captain Terrell there?'

Lepski sat up straight.

Hartley Danvaz was not only the Ballistic expert for the District Attorney, but he was also the owner of a de luxe gunsmith store that supplied the rich with every conceivable hunting weapon: a man who drew a lot of water in the City as well as being a personal friend of Lepski's Chief.

'No, Mr. Danvaz, the Chief's not in yet,' Lepski said, now wishing he hadn't taken the call. 'Anything I can do?'

'Get someone competent down here fast! I've had a break-in!' Danvaz snapped. 'Tell Captain Terrell I'd like to see him when he comes in.'

'Sure, Mr. Danvaz. I'll come myself, Mr. Danvaz,' Lepski said. 'Be right with you, Mr. Danvaz,' and he hung up.

'And that was Mr. Danvaz,' Jacoby said, keeping his face straight.

'Yeah . . . trouble. Call the Chief. Danvaz has had a break in.' Getting to his feet, Lepski shoved his chair back so violently, it fell over with a crash. 'Tell him Danvaz is yelling for him and I'm handling it,' and he was gone.

Hartley Danvaz, tall, pushing fifty-five, thin with a stoop, had the assurance and arrogance of a man worth a million.

'Who the hell are you?' he demanded as Lepski was shown into his palatial office. 'Where's Beigler?'

Lepski was in no mood to be pushed around. Maybe this jerk was a top shot, but Lepski was now 1st Grade.

'I'm Lepski,' he said in his cop voice. 'What's this about a break in?'

Danvaz squinted at him.

'Ah, yes, I've heard about you. Is Terrell coming?'

'He's been alerted. If it's only a break in, I can handle it. The Chief's busy.'

Danvaz suddenly smiled.

'Yes . . . of course.' He got to his feet. 'Come with me.'

He led the way through the big store, down some stairs to the stock room.

'They broke in here.'

Lepski looked at the small window that had been covered by a steel grille. The grille had been torn out and was hanging from its cement foundation.

'A steel cable, a hook and a car,' Lepski said. He looked through the window into a narrow alley, leading to a parking lot. 'An easy job. What did they take?'

'Was that how it was done?' Danvaz regarded Lepski with more respect. 'They took one of my best target rifles: a hand built job, complete with a telescopic sight and a silencer, worth five hundred and sixty dollars.'

'Anything else missing?'

'A box of one hundred cartridges for the gun.'

'Where was the gun kept?'

'I'll show you.'

Danvaz led the way back to the store.

'The gun was in this showcase,' he said, coming to rest beside a narrow glass box, resting on the counter. 'It was easy to get at. You just lift the glass cover. I haven't touched it. There could be finger prints.'

'Yeah. I'll get the boys down here, Mr. Danvaz and we'll cover the whole place for prints,' Lepski said, but looking at the highly polished glass case he knew this would be merely routine. The gun had been taken by someone wearing gloves.

A couple of hours later, Chief of Police Terrell, Beigler and Lepski sat around Terrell's desk, sipping coffee.

'No clues, no finger prints . . . a very professional job,' Beigler said after reading Lepski's report. 'Looks like the guy knew what he was after. There were plenty of other guns he could have taken more expensive than the one he took.'

Terrell, a heavily built man with iron grey hair, stroked his square jaw.

'The bulk of Danvaz's stock covers sporting guns: this is a target rifle. Why pick that?'

Lepski moved impatiently.

'A gun with gimmicks: the telescopic sight and the silencer. Maybe some young punk saw it in the window and got itchy fingers. Danvaz said the gun was on display a month ago in the window.'

Terrell nodded.

'Could be, but it's a killer's gun.'

'I still think it's some kid.'

'If it is, he uses professional methods,' Beigler said.

'So what? Every goddam kid who watches TV knows to use gloves, knows how to hook a grille off a window,' Lepski snorted.

'Alert the press. I don't think it will do any good, but alert them. Get them a photo of the gun ... Danvaz will certainly have one,' Terrell said.

As Lepski went to his desk and began using his telephone, Beigler said, 'Tom could be right ... could be some kid who couldn't resist stealing a gun like that.'

Terrell thought about this. He remembered when he was a teenager going every Saturday afternoon to the Danvaz store – at that time Hartley Danvaz's father had been the boss – and staring at a target rifle he yearned to own. He had yearned for it for three weeks, then suddenly the rifle had meant nothing to him. Maybe it could be some kid who had had this kind of yearning and hadn't waited.

'I hope he's right, but I don't like it. It's a killer's weapon.'

*

Dean K. McCuen was the President of the Florida Canning & Glass Corporation, a million dollar concern that supplied packaging to Florida's fruit growers. McCuen, six feet tall, iron grey hair with a whisky complexion, was a man who drove himself and his employees and achieved results. He had been married three times: each wife had left him, unable to tolerate his temper, his way of living and his demands.

McCuen lived by the clock. He rose at 07.00: spent half an hour in his gymnasium in the basement of his opulent house that stood in two acres of flowered gardens, showered at 07.31, breakfasted at 08.00, dictated until 09.00, then left at 09.3 in his Rolls-Royce for his office. This was an exact routine and never varied.

During the three years Martha Delvine had served him as his secretary she had never known him to be a second late and this bright summer morning as he came down the vast staircase to the breakfast room, she knew it was one second to 08.00 without looking at her watch.

Martha Delvine, aged thirty-six, tall, dark and without charm, was waiting at the breakfast table, the morning mail in her hand.

'Good morning, Mr. McCuen,' she said and put the mail on the table.

23

McCuen nodded. He was a man who didn't believe in superfluous words. He sat down and spread his napkin as Toko, his Japanese Man Friday, poured coffee and served scrambled eggs and lamb kidneys.

'Anything in the mail?' McCuen asked after he had munched a kidney.

'Nothing important,' Martha said. 'The usual invitations.' She paused, hesitated, then went on, 'There's one odd thing . . .'

McCuen speared another kidney, then frowned.

'Odd? Thing? What do you mean?'

She put a half sheet of cheap notepaper before him.

'This was amongst the mail.'

McCuen took out his bifocals, put them on and peered at the sheet of paper. Written in block letters was the message:

R. I. P.

09.03

THE EXECUTIONER

'What the hell is this?' McCuen demanded in a grating voice.

Toko, standing behind McCuen's chair, grimaced. From the tone of the voice he realised the morning was to begin badly.

'I don't know,' Martha said. 'I thought you should see it.'

'Why?' McCuen glared at her. 'Can't you see it's from some lunatic? Don't you know better than to bother me with this kind of thing? This is a deliberate attempt to spoil my breakfast!' He flicked the piece of paper off the table onto the floor.

'I'm sorry, Mr. McCuen.'

McCuen whirled around in his chair to glare at Toko.

'This toast is cold! What's the matter with you all this morning? Get some more!'

At 09.03, his dictation finished, his temper still smouldering, McCuen stalked out into the sunshine where his Rolls was waiting.

Brant, his middle aged, long suffering chauffeur, cap under his arm, was waiting by the car door. Martha Delvine came to the top of the imposing flight of steps to see McCuen off.

'I'll be back at six. Halliday will be coming. He said about six-thirty, but you know what he is. He can never be punctual . . .'

Those were the last words Dean K. McCuen was to utter. Martha took the horrible memory of the next second with her to her grave. She was standing close to McCuen, looking up

24

at him and she saw his high forehead turn into a spongy mess of blood and brains. A small lump of his brains splashed her face and began to ooze down her cheek. His blood sprayed her white skirt. He fell heavily, his briefcase spilling open as it hit the marble steps.

Paralysed with horror, she watched McCuen's thick set body rolling down the steps, feeling the awful, slimy thing on her face, then she began to scream.

*

Dr. Lowis, Police Medical Officer, came down the stairs to the hall, where Terrell, Beigler and Lepski waited. Lowis was a short, fat man with a balding head, freckled complexion and a talent Terrell relied on.

The call had come through as Lepski had finished alerting the press about the stolen gun. The call had been made by Steve Roberts, a prowl car officer who reported hearing screams from McCuen's residence and had investigated. His report sent Terrell, Beigler and Lepski rushing down the stairs to a Squad car, leaving Jacoby to alert the Homicide division. The report had left Terrell in no doubt that this was a murder: something that hadn't happened in Paradise City for a long time, and the murder of one of the City's more influential citizens.

They had arrived at the same time as the ambulance and Dr. Lowis had arrived five minutes later.

By now McCuen's body was on its way to the morgue.

'How is she?' Terrell asked.

'Under sedation,' Lowis told him, coming to rest at the foot of the stairs. 'You don't talk to her for at least twenty-four hours. She's half out of her head.'

Having heard the details and seen McCuen's body, Terrell could understand that.

'Any ideas, Doc?'

'A high powered rifle. I'm going back now to dig out the slug. It's my bet it was a sophisticated target rifle with a telescopic sight.'

Terrell and Beigler exchanged glances.

'How about the angle of fire?'

'From above.'

Terrell went with Lowis out onto the terrace. They surveyed the view ahead of them.

25

'From somewhere there,' Lowis said, waving his small fat hand. 'I'll get off. This is your pigeon,' and he left.

Beigler joined Terrell.

They both looked at the view. Big Chestnut trees lined the edge of McCuen's estate, beyond the trees was a highway, then space, then in the distance, a block of apartments with a flat roof.

'Some shot,' Beigler said, 'if it came from there.'

'There's nowhere else where it could have come from ... look around,' Terrell said. 'You heard what Lowis said: a sophisticated target rifle with a telescopic sight ... could be Danvaz's gun.'

'Yeah. As soon as Lowis has dug out the slug, we'll know.'

'Tom?' Terrell turned to where Lepski was waiting, 'take what men you want and cover that block of apartments. Check the roof and any empty apartment. If there are no empty apartments, check every apartment. I don't have to tell you what to do.'

'Okay, Chief.'

Lepski collected four of the Homicide squad and they went off in a car towards the distant apartment block.

'Let's go talk to the chauffeur and the Jap,' Terrell said.

'Look who's arrived,' Beigler said and groaned.

A tall, grey-haired man had driven up and was getting out of his car. Someone had once told him he looked like James Stewart, the movie actor, and from then on, he had aped the actor's mannerisms. He was Pete Hamilton, crime reporter of the *Paradise City Sun* and the City's local TV station.

'You handle him, Joe,' Terrell said out of the corner of his mouth. 'Don't tell him about the rifle. Play it dumb,' and he retreated into the house.

Herbert Brant, McCuen's chauffeur, had nothing to tell. He was still shivering with shock and Terrell quickly realised he would be wasting his time asking questions, but Toko, the Japanese servant, who hadn't seen the killing, was in complete control of himself. He handed Terrell the note that McCuen had so contemptuously flicked off the breakfast table. He built up for Terrell a picture of McCuen's habits and character. The information he gave Terrell was practicable and helpful.

Beigler was having a less happy time with Hamilton.

'Okay . . . I know it's just happened,' Hamilton said impatiently, 'but you must have an angle. McCuen is important people. He's been assassinated ... like Kennedy! Can't you see this is the biggest news story this lousy City has had in years?'

'I can see it is news,' Beigler said, feeding a strip of gum into his mouth, 'but where do you get the Kennedy angle from? Mc-Cuen isn't a U.S. President.'

'Do I get information or don't I?' Hamilton demanded.

'If I had anything to give you, Pete, you'd get it,' Beigler said blandly. 'Right now, there's nothing.'

'This target rifle reported stolen from Danvaz ... could this be the murder weapon?'

Beigler shrugged his shoulders.

'Your guess is as good as mine. We're investigating that possibility.'

'When will you have something for me?'

'About a couple of hours. We'll have a press conference at midday at headquarters.'

Hamilton regarded Beigler, his expression deadpan.

'Okay ... that's the best you can do?'

'Sure is.'

Hamilton ran down the steps to his car. Beigler watched him go, then went into the house to see how Terrell was progressing. He stood around, listening to Toko talking. When Toko had run out of steam, Terrell got rid of him. When Beigler and he were alone, Terrell showed him the note Toko had given to him.

Beigler examined it, then swore under his breath.

'A nut.'

'Could be or a cover.'

Both men knew a nut with a gun was about the trickiest killer of all killers to corner.

Beigler slid the note into a plastic envelope. 'I'll get this to the lab boys.' As he started towards his car, he paused. 'Hamilton's as hostile as ever. He's onto the stolen rifle. We're in for a lot of publicity.'

'Yes.'

Terrell made for his car.

They hadn't been gone five minutes before Pete Hamilton pulled up outside the house again. He talked to Toko, had his photographer take pictures and was driving away before the two other rival newsmen came storming up the drive.

Hamilton caught the 11.00 TV news programme. Photos of the stolen gun. McCuen's house, the distant apartment block were flashed on the screen. Hamilton told his watching audience about the note from the Executioner.

'Who is this man?' he asked. 'Is he going to strike again?'

*

The Welcome Motel stood back from Highway 4 on a dirt road, three miles outside Paradise City. Its fifteen shabby cabins, each with its own garage, was presided over by Mrs. Bertha Harris whose husband had died during the Korean war.

Bertha, large and floppily built, was now in her late fifties. The Motel provided her with a living: eating money as she called it, and since Bertha scarcely did anything else but eat, the Motel could be regarded as a success.

Usually she only expected one night stands so she was gratified and surprised when a dusty Buick had driven up the previous evening and a respectably, quiet-spoken Indian had told her he and his friends were on vacation and could they rent two cabins for a week: possibly longer?

Bertha was still more gratified when there was no haggling about the price. The Indian had agreed so readily to her terms that she wished she had asked for more. She was also gratified that the Indian had paid a week in advance for both cabins, but she was a little puzzled to see his friends were white: a young man and a girl, but then she told herself that was their affair and not hers.

The Indian signed the register as Harry Lukon and had signed the other two in as Mr. and Mrs. Jack Allen.

They had gone to the restaurant, run by Bertha's coloured help, a woolly haired negro called Sam who at the age of eighty-five still managed to keep the cabins reasonably clean and produce depressing meals when asked, which was seldom. After eating limp hamburgers and a flabby apple-pie washed down with root beer, the three had gone to their cabins and Bertha forgot about them.

At 22.00 Bertha's other three guests – elderly travelling salesmen – had gone to bed. The Motel was quiet. Poke Toholo had tapped on Chuck's cabin door and the two men had whispered together while Meg tried to hear what they were saying. Then Chuck told Meg to go to bed and he and Poke went off in the Buick, heading for Paradise City.

By the confident way he drove once they reached the City,

Chuck could tell Poke knew the place like the back of his hand. It was only after they had driven around one of the shopping blocks a couple of times that Poke explained what they were about to do.

He had everything organised. Under the back seat of the car was a steel hook and a length of steel cable. It had been child's play to rip off the grille that protected the stock room window of the gunsmith's store.

While Chuck, sweating slightly and nervous, had kept watch in the dark alley, Poke had slid through the window. A minute or so later, he had handed out a target rifle, a telescopic sight and a box containing a silencer. Chuck took these articles from him and put them under the seat of the car.

They had driven back to the Motel.

'Go to bed,' Poke said as he pulled up outside Chuck's cabin. 'Don't tell her a thing . . . understand?'

Chuck got out of the car.

'What are you going to do?'

'You'll know,' Poke said quietly and drove away into the darkness.

Chuck found Meg in bed, awake and waiting for him anxiously.

'Where have you been?' she asked, watching him undress.

He slid into the big bed beside her and reached for her.

'Where have you been?' she repeated, wrestling with him. 'Don't mess me around. You haven't washed, you pig! You haven't even cleaned your teeth!'

'Who cares?' Chuck said and forced her on her back.

They slept until 09.50. As Meg was heating coffee, she saw through the window, Poke drive up and put the car in the garage.

'Has he been out all night?' she asked, pouring the coffee into cups.

'Why don't you ask him?' Chuck said.

That silenced her.

Later, Chuck shaved and took a shower while Meg watched the commercials on TV.

As Chuck was soaping himself he wondered about Poke. He thought of the gun. Poke had been out all night. There were to be three killings, he had said. Uneasily, Chuck wondered if Poke had used the gun already.

It was while he was combing his hair that Pete Hamilton

came on the screen to tell about McCuen's murder. He was talking about the note that McCuen had received as Chuck came out of the shower room.

'Listen to this,' Meg said excitedly.

'So there's a killer in our midst ... possibly a lunatic killer,' Hamilton was saying. 'A man who calls himself The Executioner. What is his motive? Will he kill again? Last night, a high powered target rifle was stolen from the well known gunsmith's store ... Danvaz Guns. Was the stolen rifle the weapon that killed McCuen? Here is the photograph of the gun which is fitted with a telescopic sight and a silencer.' The picture changed to show the rifle and Chuck flinched.

Hamilton went on, 'Look carefully at this picture. If you have seen this gun before, if you have seen anyone with such a gun, then call Police Headquarters immediately. Dean K. McCuen was one of our best known citizens. He ...'

Chuck turned off the set.

'Who cares?' he said, trying to make his voice sound casual. 'Let's go look at the town.'

Meg was staring at him. He had lost colour and there were sweat beads on his forehead and his eyes were shifty. She felt a chill run up her spine.

'What's the matter?'

Chuck put on his shirt.

'Matter? Nothing's the matter! Don't you want to take a look at the town?'

'This murder ... this man ... The Executioner ... it's nothing to do with us, is it, Chuck?'

Chuck pulled on his trousers.

'You nuts or something? To do with *us*?'

He didn't meet her eyes.

'Then why are you looking like that? It *is* something to do with us!' Meg retreated away from him. 'Why was he out all night? Where's all this money he's promising coming from?'

Chuck knew this was a moment of crisis. This was a now or never situation.

'Okay!' he said, his voice savage. 'Pack your things! You were warned! You were told not to ask questions ... now, you're out! Go on! Pack your goddamn things! You're out!'

Meg cringed and waved her hands helplessly at him.

'No! Come with me, Chuck: He's bad! I know it! Come with me!'

'You heard what I said! Pack! You're out!'

She sat on the unmade bed, her head in her hands.

'I can't be alone, Chuck ... all right ... forget it. I won't ask questions. I don't want to go.'

With his ear pressed against the flimsy wooden wall of his cabin, Poke Toholo listened.

Chuck knew he had won but this was the time to drive it home to her.

'I'm getting sick of you,' he said. 'There are plenty of girls I can find. You'd better clear out. Go on ... pack!'

She was now almost grovelling.

'Please, Chuck ... I don't care. I won't ask any more questions. I just have to stay with you!'

He walked around the room, as if in doubt.

'I'll talk to Poke. He'll have to hear about this. I think you should get the hell out of here.'

Meg jumped up and caught hold of his arm.

'No, don't tell him. I promise! I swear I won't ask any more questions! I'll do what you tell me! I promise!'

Chuck made as if he was hesitating, then he nodded.

'Okay, so I'll forget it. Let's go look at the town, huh?'

'Yes.' She looked gratefully at him. 'Yes, please.'

'I'll ask Poke if we can take the car.'

Immediately she was in a panic again.

'You won't tell him ... you won't say anything to him?'

His grin was gloating. It was a sop to his ego that she should grovel before him.

'I won't tell him.' He caught hold of her chin between his short, sweaty fingers and pinched it, making her wince. 'But remember, baby, this is your last chance.'

He left the cabin and tapped on Poke's door. Poke let him in. The two men looked at each other as Poke closed the door.

'I heard it all,' he said softly. 'You handled it right. Take her in the car to the beach. Keep her occupied. I'm going to sleep.' He took from his hip pocket a twenty dollar bill. 'Take this ... get her quieted down.' He paused. His black glittering eyes searched Chuck's face. 'I'll need you tonight. We leave here at 11 o'clock.'

Chuck stiffened and his mouth turned dry.

'The second one?'

Poke nodded.

31

Chuck looked away as he said, 'You handled the first one by yourself. Why do you want me?'

'I need you this time,' Poke said. 'Take her to the beach and give her a good time.'

Chuck nodded, hesitated, then left the cabin.

Poke closed the door after him and shot the bolt. He waited until Chuck and Meg had driven away in the Buick, then he went to his bed, lifted the mattress and took from its hiding place the target rifle.

Sitting on the edge of the bed, he began to clean it.

*

It was a little after 14.00 before Terrell had read through all the reports that had been coming to his desk during the morning. He had left Beigler to cope with the in-coming calls. Hamilton's television story had sparked off an explosion in the City that kept the telephone bells at headquarters continually ringing. The rich of the City were spoilt people and they were highly nervous. They regarded the police force as their servants: a force created entirely for their protection. What were the police doing about this lunatic? they demanded angrily, shrilly and even tearfully. Didn't the police realise this man could kill again? What was being done?

Beigler coped with these calls in his stolid, reassuring way: a cigarette never out of his mouth and a carton of coffee at his side.

Listening to the various voices hammering against his ear drum he thought Hamilton had really started something and his foot itched to connect with Hamilton's backside.

Lawson Hedley, the Mayor of the City, was a man of sense. He had already talked to Terrell.

'Could be a nut,' Terrell had said. 'Could be a blind. Until I get more information, I can't give you a picture. I'll have my reports sorted out around 15.00. If you want to sit in on it, Lawson, I'll be glad to have you.'

'I'll be there, Frank. It's too bad this goddam Hamilton has started this scare before we know what it's all about. I'll be around.'

At 15.00 Terrell, Hedley and Beigler sat down around Terrell's desk.

'The killer's gun was stolen from Danvaz's store last night,'

Terrell said. 'The ballistic report confirms this. The killer fired the shot from the Connaught apartment block, from the penthouse terrace. As you know, the penthouse is owned by Tom Davis and as you know, he is somewhere on vacation in Europe. He's been away now for three months and it looks like the killer knew this. The elevator goes from the basement garage right into the apartment. With the right tool, it's not so hard to take the elevator up there. It was an easy job. The killer drove into the garage, got into Davis's apartment, went out onto the terrace and waited for McCuen to show. The janitor of the Connaught is up and around at 06.00. I'd say the killer arrived sometime in the night and waited. The janitor had breakfast at 09.30. The place is unguarded from 09.30 until 10.15. That's when the killer left.'

Hedley ran his hand over his thinning hair.

'Sounds to me as if this man had this carefully planned and planned a long time ago.'

'Maybe or he was familiar with the routine. I'm inclined to think he knew just when to shoot and when to leave and he must have known that Davis was away.'

'So he's a local man?'

'Looks like it.'

Hedley moved restlessly.

'What else have you got?'

'There's this note ... an odd thing. It's a warning. It was posted last night. I don't understand it. He's warning McCuen he'll be killed. Why?'

'Publicity,' Beigler said. 'He's certainly got it.'

'Maybe. Well, as you say, he's got it. The lab boys have worked the note over. No finger prints, written with a ball pen, the paper you can find in any cheap store. This gives us nothing but the message.' Terrell produced the note and handed it to Hedley. 'The writing is printed as you see and badly formed. The important thing is the time on the note, 09.03. The killer had inside information about McCuen's habits. He must have known McCuen was a crank about time. He must have known McCuen always left his house at 09.03. As far as I can find out the only people who would know this exact time are McCuen's secretary, his chauffeur and his servant. They're not involved. I'm sure of that. It's possible McCuen boasted to his friends about his exactness of time. That I'm going to check. It's reasonable to assume the killer lives here or has lived here and he knows a lot about the habits of the people who do live here: the fact he knew Davis was on vacation, what time the janitor has breakfast and McCuen always left his house at exactly 09.03. That helps us a little, but not much. I don't have to tell you about McCuen. He wasn't particularly liked and he had a lot of business enemies. I'm damned if I can believe any of his business associates would go gunning for him, but I could be wrong. This note could be a smoke screen, but I have a feeling it's not. My hunch is we are dealing with a nut with a grudge: someone who lives here and someone we're going to hear from again.'

Hedley absorbed all this, then he asked, 'So what's the next move?'

Terrell leaned forward, resting his big hands on his desk.

'Strictly between ourselves, I wish I knew. There is no immediate next move. Of course we will give out we are handling it, making inquiries and so on and so on, but there isn't much we can do. We'll keep the photo of the rifle before the public, we will dig into McCuen's life and talk to his friends, but I don't think any of this will get us far. An apparently motiveless killing like this one is a real toughie. We'll have to wait and hope it's only an isolated killing.'

Hedley stiffened.

'Are you suggesting this man could do it again?'

'Ask yourself. I hope not. We'll be going through the motions. We'll check on everyone who has quarrelled with McCuen and there are a lot of them. We'll try to find out if anyone had a real grudge against him ... maybe one of his employees. If you have any ideas, Lawson, now's the time to trot them out.'

Hedley crushed out his cigar in the ash tray and stood up.

'No ... I understand the position. All right, keep trying, Frank. I'll get back to my office and start pouring oil ... that's the least I can do.'

When he had gone, Terrell finished his coffee, lit his pipe and looked at Beigler.

'Let's get moving, Joe ... the works. Get them all at it. I don't think they'll come up with anything, but we've got to do something.'

'Yeah.' Beigler got to his feet. 'You think there'll be another, Chief?'

'I hope not.'

'I think there will. We have a nut on our hands.' Beigler

shook his head. 'Lucky Fred. I wouldn't mind being in hospital with a broken leg right now.'

'He'll make a mistake . . . they always do,' Terrell said without much conviction in his voice.

'But when?'

'That's right . . . when.'

They looked at each other, then Beigler went into the Detectives' room to get his men working.

*

Aware at this time in the evening his neighbours would be out in their gardens attacking aphis with their D.D.T. guns or cutting their lawns, Lepski decided to stage an entrance that would set them up on their ears.

He roared down the avenue in his car at fifty miles an hour, then stood on his brake pedal as he reached his garden gate, bringing the car to a screeching halt and nearly throwing himself through the windshield. If anything, Lepski was a show off, but maybe, he thought as he flung himself out of the car, that sudden stop had been a little too spectacular for safety. Slamming the car door, aware his neighbours had suspended all activity and were staring at him with round eyes, he pounded up the garden path to his front door. Stabbing the key into the lock, he decided the scene was going well. Everyone living down the street had by now been told by Lepski's wife about his promotion. Now was the time to show all these squares a 1st Grade Detective in action.

Unfortunately he was trying to unlock his front door with his car key. If he could have swept into the house, slamming the door, the impression he had made would have been long discussed, but this frustrated fiddling at the lock until he realised he was using the wrong key spoilt the scene.

As he groped, swearing, for the right key, the front door jerked open.

'Do you have to drive like that?' Carroll Lepski asked severely. 'Don't you realise you're setting a bad example?'

Lepski barged past her, kicked the door shut and headed for the bathroom.

'I'm breaking my neck for a pee,' he announced, then slammed the door.

Carroll sighed. Aged twenty-seven, tall, dark and pretty she had a will of her own. Before marrying Lepski, she had been a clerk in the American Express Company in Miami dealing with the rich, arranging their affairs and advising them. The work had given her a lot of self-confidence and made her somewhat bossy.

She regarded her husband as the best and smartest detective at headquarters. She planned, in probably six or possibly seven years time to see him as Chief of Police. This again she didn't tell him, but she nagged him from promotion to promotion. He was now 1st Grade: the next move was to be Sergeant.

Lepski came out of the bathroom, dramatically wiping non-existent sweat from his face.

'Let's have a drink,' he said, throwing himself into a chair. 'I've only got five minutes . . . just time to change my shirt.'

'If you're on duty again, Lepski, you don't drink! I'll get you a Coke.'

'I want a goddamn drink . . . a big whisky with lots of ice!'

She went into the kitchen and brought him a large Coke with lots of ice.

'What are you so worked up about?' she asked, sitting on the arm of a chair.

'Me? I'm not worked up! What makes you think I'm worked up?' He drank half the Coke and grimaced. 'How about putting a slug of Scotch in this?'

'No! You look and act like you're worked up. I'm worked up too. I've been glued to the television. This killer . . . The Executioner . . . what's happening?'

'A nut. I don't have to tell you: a nut's the worst headache we can get. Now listen, Carroll, not a word to anyone! I know all your harpy friends imagine they'll get first hand news from you, but don't tell them a thing!'

'There's nothing to tell, is there? An idiot child would know this man is a nutter. What's going on? Have you found him yet?'

Lepski released a hollow laugh.

'Not yet. I'll be out all night making goddam inquiries. Routine stuff. The City's scared. We have to look busy, but it's just a waste of time, but don't tell anyone.'

'I have a clue, Lepski.' Now Carroll had an admission that her husband was up against a blank wall she was ready to steer him to further promotion. 'As soon as I heard Hamilton on TV

this morning, I went around to Mehitabel Bessinger. I felt sure
if anyone could crack this case it'd be her.'

Lepski stiffened, then loosened his collar.

'That old fake? You're crazy! Now, look, baby, get me a clean
shirt. I'll be out all night. How about cutting me a couple of
sandwiches? What have we got in the fridge? Is there any of
that beef left?'

'Listen to me, Lepski,' Carroll said firmly. 'Mehitabel may
be old, but she isn't a fake. She has powers. I told her how important this was to you and . . .'

'Wait a minute!' Lepski sat forward, suspicion on his face.
'Did you give her my whisky?' Jumping to his feet, he rushed
to the liquor cabinet. His bottle of Cutty Sark was missing. He
turned and looked accusingly at his wife. 'You gave that drunken old bag my whisky!'

'Mehitabel is not a drunken old bag! Naturally she likes a
drink from time to time. Yes, I gave her the whisky . . . anyway,
Lepski, I think you drink too much.'

Lepski dragged his tie loose.

'Never mind how much I drink! You mean . . .'

'Be quiet! I want you to listen!' Carroll's voice rose.

'Oh, sure, sure.' Lepski ran his fingers through his hair. 'You
don't have to tell me.' He took off his tie and began to scrumple
it in his hands. 'You went to her and she got her goddamn crystal ball out and for a bottle of my best whisky, she told you who
killed McCuen . . . right?'

Carroll squared her shoulders.

'That's just what she did. This could be the quick break
through. Mehitabel saw the killer in her crystal ball.'

Lepski made a noise like a pneumatic drill as he threw his tie
on the floor and stamped on it.

'You don't have to show off,' Carroll said coldly. 'There are
times when I think you have the mentality of a spoilt child.'

Lepski closed his eyes but finally got control of himself.

'Yeah . . . you could be right. Fine . . . now let's forget about
Mehitabel. Suppose you cut me some sandwiches? I'd like some
of that beef . . . if there's any left.'

'You think too much about food,' Carroll said. 'Will you
please pay attention? Mehitabel saw this man! He's an Indian.
He was wearing a flowered shirt and there were two other people
with him: a man and a woman, but she couldn't see them
clearly.'

37

'Is that right?' Lepski sneered. 'That doesn't surprise me. Once that old rum-dum gets her hands on a bottle she can't see anything clearly.' He got to his feet. 'I'm taking a shave and I'm changing my shirt. Will you get those sandwiches ready?'

Carroll pounded her knees with her fists. There were times – and this was one of them – when she could be as dramatic as Lepski.

'But can't you see, you idiot, this is a clue ... a vital clue?' she said furiously. 'Why must you be so narrow minded? I know Mehitabel is old, but she has powers ... she's a medium.'

'Did you call me an idiot?' Lepski said, drawing himself up.

'Did you hear what I was saying?' Carroll blazed, her eyes flashing.

'I heard you call me an idiot,' Lepski said. 'I'm going to change my shirt. If there's any beef left, I'd like some sandwiches,' and he stalked off to their bedroom.

Carroll was waiting with a pack of sandwiches as Lepski, shaved, showered and in a fresh shirt, came out of the bedroom.

He looked at the pack of sandwiches as Carroll thrust them at him.

'Beef?'

'Oh God! Yes!'

'Mustard?'

'Yes.'

He smiled.

'See you sometime, honey. Just forget about that old rum-dum.' He aimed a kiss at her cheek, then stormed down the garden path to his car.

He was to spend a wasteful night tramping the streets asking questions, visiting nightclubs to which McCuen belonged, but getting a picture, as did the other questioning detectives, that fear was gripping the City : fear like an atomic fall out.

Three

Detective 2nd Grade Max Jacoby was catching the midnight stint. While he guarded the telephone, he was busy classifying the mass of reports on the McCuen murder that were continually coming in, sorting the wheat from the chaff for Terrell's eyes the first thing the following morning.

Two young police officers kept him company: smart men but without much experience. The red head was Dusty Lucas: the squat one was Rocky Hamblin. They were yawning over more reports.

'These guys sure wear out shoe leather,' Dusty observed, reaching for another report. 'Imagine: this is my forty-third report and what does it say: nothing!'

Aware, as their senior, he had to set an example, Jacoby looked up and scowled. 'This is police work. The forty-fourth report could give us what we're looking for.'

'Oh, yeah?' Both Rookies exclaimed. 'Who are you trying to kid, Max?'

Then the telephone bell rang.

As Jacoby reached for the receiver, he looked at the fly blown wall clock. The time was 22.47.

'Police headquarters: Jacoby,' he said briskly.

'I want help here,' a man said. His voice was unsteady but authoritative. 'The Seagull, Beach Drive. Send someone quickly.'

'Who is this talking?' Jacoby asked as he scribbled the address on a pad.

'Malcolm Riddle. I have a dead woman here ... send someone quickly.'

Jacoby was familiar with the names of the more important citizens of the city. Malcolm Riddle was the President of the Yacht Club, the Chairman of the Opera House and his wife was considered to be the seventh richest woman in Florida. That made him important.

'Yes, Mr. Riddle.' Jacoby sat forward in his chair. 'An officer will be with you right away.' He was already looking at the electronic chart that told him where the prowl cars were. 'Can you give me more details?'

'It's murder,' Riddle said flatly and broke the connection.

Within seconds Jacoby was in contact with Patrol Officer Steve Roberts who was covering the area near Beach Drive.

'Get over to The Seagull, Beach Drive fast, Steve,' he said. 'Malcolm Riddle is reporting a murder. I'll alert Homicide. Just hold everything until they arrive.'

'Sure,' Roberts said, a startled note in his voice. 'I'm on my way.'

For the next few minutes Jacoby was busy on the phone, watched by the two pop-eyed Rookies. He first called Beigler who was just going to bed. Beigler listened and when he heard Malcolm Riddle was involved, he told Jacoby to alert Terrell.

'Where's Lepski?' Beigler asked, struggling with a yawn.

'He should be home by now. He clocked out twenty minutes ago.'

'Get him down there,' Beigler said and hung up.

Beigler and Lepski arrived simultaneously at the small luxe bungalow.

The bungalow was so obviously a love nest that no one looking beyond the discreet flowering shrubs that half screened the little place could have had any other ideas about it. It faced the sea, had a forest of mangrove trees protecting its rear and tall, over-grown flowering shrubs protecting its flanks.

Roberts' prowl car was parked under a palm tree. The big, rubbery faced cop came out of the shadows and joined Beigler.

'I took a look, sarg,' he said, 'then left it. You'll love this ... it's the Executioner again.'

Beigler swore under his breath, then walked up the short path to the open front door. He gestured to Lepski and Roberts to stay where they were.

He found Malcolm Riddle sitting in a lounging chair in the big living-room. Riddle was a heavily built man in his late fifties: his sun tanned, fleshy face was handsome enough for him to be mistaken for a film star. There was a look of dead despair on his face that shocked Beigler. He knew Riddle and liked him and knew about his difficulties. He knew Riddle's wife was a bitch. Allowing for the fact that after a riding accident she had now to spend her life in a wheel chair, she still remained a bitch.

Riddle looked up as Beigler came into the room.

'Ah, Joe ... glad it's you. This is a hell of a mess.' He waved towards a far door. 'She's in there.'

'Take it easy, Mr. Riddle,' Beigler said gently and went to

40

the door that led into the bedroom. The lights were on. The king sized bed took up most of the floor space.

The woman lay face down on the bed, naked. Beigler's practised eyes saw the rope of nylon stocking around her throat, and then his eyes shifted to her long, sun tanned back.

From the base of her neck to the base of her buttocks was painted in glistening black paint the legend:

THE EXECUTIONER

Beigler stood for a long moment, staring at the body, his face hard and set, then he walked through the sitting-room, ignoring Riddle and out into the hot night air.

'It's our boy again,' he said to Lepski. 'Set it up. Get the squad down here. I'm taking Riddle out of here.'

Lepski nodded and using the car's telephone, he called headquarters.

Beigler returned to the bungalow.

'The press will be swarming around here any time now,' he said. 'Let me take you home, Mr. Riddle.'

Riddle got heavily to his feet.

'I don't want to go home ... just yet. Of course you want to question me. I'll take my car ... you follow me. We'll go down to Mala Bay ... it'll be quiet there.'

Ten minutes later, Riddle parked his car under a palm tree. Mala Bay was a day time favourite for beach lovers, but at night, it was always deserted.

Beigler joined him and the two men sat side by side on the sand. There was a long pause, then Riddle said, 'This is a mess, isn't it? It's the end of the road for me. Why did that bastard pick on me?' He accepted Beigler's cigarette and both men lit up. 'If I hadn't had a flat tyre this wouldn't have happened. It's fate, I suppose. I've always got to the bungalow before Lisa did, but tonight, I had this flat and she was there ahead of me.'

'Would you fill me in, Mr. Riddle?' Beigler said. 'It'll all have to come out. I'm sorry. I need everything you can give me. This nut could kill again.'

'Yes ... go ahead ... ask what you like.'

'Who's the woman?'

'Lisa Mendoza.' Riddle stared at the glowing tip of his cigarette. 'You know about my wife. Of course I should not have done it, but I'm not getting any younger ... call it a last fling. I ran into Lisa. Something sparked off between us. She was a lovely person and lonely like myself.' His voice became unsteady and he paused. 'There it is. I bought the bungalow. It was our love nest ... that's what the tabloids will call it, won't they?'

'Did you have the bungalow long?'

'Eighteen months ... nineteen months ... something like that. Both of us knew it couldn't last ... what does?'

'How often did you meet?'

'Every Friday night. It was a fixed thing ... like this Friday night.'

'She didn't live at the bungalow?'

'Good God, no! We only used it on Friday nights. She has her own home. We chose Friday as my wife always goes to bed early on that night. We entertain on Saturdays and she needs extra rest.'

'Who knew about this arrangement, Mr. Riddle? I mean apart from you and Miss Mendoza.'

Riddle looked blankly at him.

'Knew?'

'Did you confide in anyone ... any of your friends?'

'What an odd question.'

Beigler restrained his impatience.

'It's not so odd. You're preoccupied with what has happened to you. I'm preoccupied with a killer who has killed twice and could kill again. He knew McCuen's habits. It looks to me he also knew your habits. Was this association of yours a secret? Did you confide in anyone?'

Riddle crushed out his cigarette in the sand as he thought.

'Yes ... I understand. I'm sorry. I'm being selfish. I see what you're getting at. Yes, I did confide in a few of my very close friends, but they wouldn't ...'

'I'm not saying they did, but maybe through them there was a leak. Could I know who they are?'

Riddle rubbed his forehead.

'There is Harriet Green: she's my secretary. She leased the bungalow. Then David Bentley: I sail with him: he's my closest friend. Terry Thompson: he's the manager of the Opera House. He was Lisa's friend. He knew and approved.' He paused, thinking. 'Luke Williams: he was my alibi for Friday nights. We were supposed to be at a bowling alley. My wife approved of this. She thought the exercise was good for me.'

In the brilliant moonlight, Beigler scribbled down the names in his notebook.

'You said you had a flat tyre?'

'Yes ... I went to get my car and found the off side front tyre was flat. Bates, my chauffeur, was off duty so I changed the tyre myself. I'm not good at this kind of chore and it took time. Usually I get to the bungalow at nine o'clock. I wasn't worried. I knew Lisa would wait for me. I got to the bungalow thirty-five minutes late. I found her. That's it. Anything else?'

Beigler hesitated. Was it possible, he asked himself, that Riddle had quarrelled with the woman and had killed her? Could he have painted the word on her back to shift suspicion from himself? But looking at the tragic face, he was satisfied.

'No, go home, Mr. Riddle.' He got to his feet. 'The Chief will want to see you. I'll get a couple of men over to your place right away to keep the press off you.'

'Thanks.' Riddle stood up. He turned to look at Beigler. 'It's a mess, isn't it?' He hesitated, then offered his hand. A little surprised, Beigler took it. 'Thanks for being so understanding.'

'It'll work out,' Beigler said.

'Yes.'

Riddle turned, got in his car and drove away.

Beigler grimaced. Then with a shake of his head, he got in his car and headed back to the bungalow.

*

Alone in the small, stuffy cabin, Poke Toholo listened to the commentator on the small screen. Chuck and Meg were out. He had told Chuck to take Meg dancing and to keep her out late.

The fat, excited looking man with the love nest as his background was waving his microphone as he talked. A few moments ago, Lisa Mendoza's body, covered by a sheet, had been brought out of the bungalow on a stretcher and the stretcher had been fed into the waiting ambulance.

'So the Executioner strikes again,' the commentator said dramatically. 'First Dean K. McCuen, one of our best known citizens, shot to death yesterday, now Lisa Mendoza, known to music lovers of this City as a fine violinist, has been strangled and her body defiled by the killer's signature. There is no one in our City this night who isn't asking the same question: not if this lunatic will strike again, but *when* will he strike again and *who* will be his next victim. I have with me Chief of Police Terrell...'

Poke smiled. The atmosphere was building up beautifully, he thought. He listened to Terrell's plea against panic, knowing the rich and the spoilt would not be reassured. It would need now only one more killing for real stark panic, so necessary to his plan, to have the City in his grip.

Chuck must be more closely involved this time, Poke thought. Up to now, Chuck's only contribution had been to help steal the rifle and to let the air out of Riddle's tyre. That had been necessary to give Poke time to reach the bungalow and to find the woman there on her own. But the next killing would be different. It was time Chuck earned the promised money: time for him to be so involved, he couldn't rat.

Poke's attention was drawn back to the lighted screen.

The commentator was now whispering with a man who had joined him. Poke heard the commentator whisper, 'For God's sake! Are you sure?'

The other man nodded and moved out of the camera's range.

The commentator mopped his sweating face with his handkerchief as he faced the camera.

'Folks ... I've just heard Mr. Malcolm Riddle is dead. This will shock you as it shocks me. While driving back to his home, after being interviewed by the police, Mr. Riddle apparently lost control of his car. The car plunged over the cliff into the sea at West Point. Mr. Riddle...'

Poke got to his feet and stretched. It was building up even better than he had hoped. He looked at his watch. The time now was a few minutes after midnight. He turned off the television set, then taking off his flowered shirt and dropping his blue hipsters, he went into the shower room. Some minutes later, he put on faded red pyjamas and lay on the bed. He turned off the light.

His mind went back to the moment when he had broken into the bungalow. The lock on the back door had offered no resistance. He had waited in the darkness. She had arrived at 21.25 as he knew she would from Luke Williams whispered conversation with another Club member at the bar while Poke was serving them drinks. He was standing behind the drapes in the big bedroom. He watched her undress. She had tossed her stockings carelessly from her and they had landed within a foot of where he was hiding. He had meant to use his hands, but as she had supplied the weapon, he had accepted it.

The sound of a car driving into the garage broke his thoughts. He slid off the bed and peered through the curtains.

Chuck and Meg were walking to their cabin. He heard the door slam and then listened to the murmur of their voices.

He stretched out on the bed again.

Tomorrow . . . the final killing . . . then the harvest.

He lay awake for some time, thinking. It was working out exactly the way he had planned. In a week the money would begin to come in.

He was still thinking about the money as he drifted off into sleep.

*

Lights burned in Mayor Hedley's penthouse on the top of City Hall.

The time was 02.33.

Hedley had just got rid of Pete Hamilton and five other pressmen. They had given him a roasting that left him furious, white faced and sweating.

His wife, Monica, a forty-three-year-old motherly type of woman, sensible and nice, sat in a chair away from him. Chief of Police Terrell sat in a chair facing him.

'Lawson, dear, you must try to calm yourself,' Monica said soothingly. 'It's not good for you to get so worked up. You know . . .'

'Calm myself?' Hedley's voice exploded, 'calm myself! Don't you realise this goddamn thing could lose me my job? Calm myself you say! With a lunatic killer loose in this City!'

Monica and Terrell exchanged glances.

'But honey if you did happen to lose your job, would it matter so much?'

Hedley clenched his fists and sucked in a breath of exasperation.

'You don't understand. Monica . . . please go to bed. I want to talk to Frank.'

'But I do understand, Lawson.'

'You don't! What you don't seem able to grasp is the whole City is exploding!'

'Is it?' She got up and walked gracefully to the big picture window and looked at the residential skyscrapers that surroun-

45

ded City Hall. Only a few lights showed in the many windows. 'I would say most folk are in bed and asleep. The only people exploding as far as I can see are a handful of pressmen and you.'

'Monica, will you please go to bed!'

'Yes, of course.' She smiled at Terrell, then made her way to the door. 'Lawson is very civic minded, Frank,' she said at the door, then she was gone.

There was a long pause, Hedley said, 'Monica doesn't appreciate the implications behind all this. I don't have to tell you, you and I could be out of office tomorrow, do I?'

Terrell took out his pipe and began to fill it.

'Could we?' He regarded Hedley. 'I've been waiting to tell you something, Lawson. Now Monica isn't with us, I'll say it. In my view, you're acting like an old woman who thinks there is a man under her bed.'

Hedley flushed red.

'Are you talking to me?' he demanded, then under Terrell's steady stare, he managed to control his temper. 'You can't say a thing like that to me!'

'I've said it,' Terrell said mildly. 'Now, for a change, listen to me.' He paused to light his pipe, then when it was going to his satisfaction, he went on, 'I've been Chief of Police for fifteen years. I've done a job and I know it as you know it. Just because we have a nut loose who has killed two people there's no cause to panic and that is what you are doing. You should know as I know every so often a City gets a nut. This is nothing unique.'

Hedley pressed his finger tips to his forehead.

'But this is happening to Paradise City!'

'That's right. What's so special about Paradise City? I'll tell you. Paradise City is the playground of some of the richest, most arrogant, most vulgar and most unpleasant people in this country. So a killer arrives: a fox among the golden geese. If it happened in any other City you wouldn't bother to read about it.'

Trying to keep his voice steady, Hedley said, 'It's my duty to protect the people I serve! I don't give a damn what happens in any other City! It's what happens here that counts!'

'So what is happening here? A nut has killed two people. Getting into a panic won't find him.'

'You sit there and talk,' Hedley said angrily, 'but what are you doing?'

'I'll find him. It'll take time, but I'll find him. Right now, by the way you and the press are behaving I get the idea you and they are creating an atmosphere the killer wants.'

Hedley reared back in his chair.

'What do you mean? Be careful what you're saying! So far you and your men haven't done a goddam thing to impress anyone! Two killings! And what have you got? Nothing! What do you mean by saying I'm creating an atmosphere this lunatic wants? Just what the hell do you mean by saying a thing like that?'

Completely unruffled, Terrell crossed one thick leg over the other.

'I've lived in this City most of my life,' he said. 'For the first time I smell fear. I have smelt money, sex, corruption, scandal and vice, but never fear . . . I'm smelling it now.'

Hedley made a gesture of exasperation.

'I don't give a damn about that! You're accusing me of making an atmosphere this killer wants . . . you'd better explain!'

'Have you asked yourself what is the motive behind these killings?' Terrell asked. 'Why this killer publicises himself? When I have a murder case on my hands, I ask myself what is the motive? Without a motive, a killing is tough to solve. So I have asked myself what is the motive behind these two killings?'

Hedley dropped back in his chair.

'Why look at me? This is your job, goddamn it!'

'That's right. It is my job.' Terrell puffed at his pipe. 'No murder is ever committed without a motive. When dealing with a nut, the motive is obscure, but it is there, if you look for it hard enough. McCuen was a typical product of this City. Lisa Mendoza was a musician. There is no connection between these two except one thing: their deaths are the means to publicise a man who calls himself the Executioner. It's a clever name . . . a name that makes an impact. With a name like that, he gets headlines. With a name like that, he has started a panic in this City. Until I find something else, I think that is the motive . . . to create panic in this City.'

'Oh, nonsense!' Hedley snapped. 'Why should a nut want to create a panic?'

'That's what he is doing,' Terrell said quietly. 'I'm not saying I'm right, but with nothing else to go on, and looking at the scene, this could be the motive.'

47

Hedley thought for a long moment, then pushed back his chair.

'I'm tired. I've had enough for tonight. I'm sorry I blew up, Frank. All right ... I'll go along with your thinking. I don't have to tell you what tomorrow is going to be like.' As Terrell said nothing, Hedley paused as he thought of tomorrow's newspapers, the non-stop ringing of his telephone bell and Pete Hamilton creating trouble on the 10.00 TV news. 'You really think this nut is trying to throw a scare into this City?'

'He's doing it, isn't he?'

'So what are we going to do?'

'That now depends on you,' Terrell said. He leaned forward and knocked out his pipe in the ash tray. 'Before I return to headquarters I want to know if you are still on my side.'

'On your side?' Hedley stared at him. 'Of course I am!'

'Are you?' Terrell looked woodenly at Hedley. 'A moment ago you were talking about me losing my job. Do you want a new Chief of Police?'

Hedley flinched.

'Why the hell should I want a new Chief of Police? If there's anyone who can catch this bastard it's you!'

Terrell got to his feet.

'That's right. If there's anyone who can catch him it's me. So let's cut out the panic.'

'That's telling him, Frank,' Monica said from the open doorway. 'And how he needed to be told!'

Both men turned, realising only at this moment that she had been listening all the time.

Hedley suddenly relaxed. He looked sheepish.

'Wives! You want to take her off my hands, Frank?'

Terrell relaxed too. He winked at Monica.

'If I hadn't one of my own, I'd take you up on that,' he said. 'Both of them are as good as each other.' He started towards the door.

Hedley said, hesitation in his voice, 'Do you want me at headquarters tomorrow?'

'You're always wanted, Lawson,' Terrell said, pausing. He touched Monica's hand, then taking the elevator, he went down to face the waiting TV cameras.

*

Jack Anders, doorman of the Plaza Beach hotel, stood on the red carpet before the imposing marble portals that led into the best hotel in the City, his keen grey eyes surveying the boulevard, his big hands clasped behind his back.

Anders was a 2nd World War veteran, the holder of a number of impressive combat medals and was now a recognised character on the boulevard. He had been doorman of the Plaza Beach hotel for the past twenty years.

This was the slack time in the morning so Anders was taking it easy. In another couple of hours cars would be arriving for the pre-lunch cocktail hour and he would be fully occupied opening car doors, instructing chauffeurs where to park, tipping his peak cap to the regulars, answering idiotic questions, giving information and collecting dollar bills. None of the Plaza Beach hotel's clients ever dreamed of speaking to Anders without parting with a dollar bill. But at this hour of 09.30, he didn't expect any demands on his attention and accordingly was relaxing.

Police Officer Paddy McNeil, a massively built, elderly Irishman who was around to take care of any traffic snarl up on the boulevard and generally to keep an eye on the aged and the rich, came to rest beside Anders.

The two men were friends. Their friendship had grown over the years while Anders had stood sentinel in all weathers outside the hotel and while McNeil paced the boulevard and came around to the hotel every two hours to pause and exchange greetings.

'How's your pal ... the Executioner?' Anders asked as McNeil paused by his side. 'I was listening to the radio. Got all my old dears wetting their knickers.'

'Your old dears aren't the only ones,' McNeil said darkly. 'Right now life isn't worth living. I'm thankful to be on patrol. Except for a dozen of us old deadbeats, the rest of us are out looking for his sonofabitch. Two truck loads of men from Miami arrived this morning. So much water down a drain. What do the finks from Miami know about this City?'

'Do you think what Hamilton says is right?' Anders asked innocently. He liked needling McNeil.

'Hamilton?' McNeil snorted. 'I never listen to that big mouth ... he's a trouble maker.' He cocked an eye at Anders. 'What did he say?'

'That this killer is a homicidal maniac with a grudge against the rich.'

McNeil pushed his cap forward to scratch the back of his head.

'You don't have to be either homicidal or a maniac to hate the rich,' he said after some thought. 'I can't say I love the rich myself.'

Anders concealed a grin. 'They have their uses.'

'You can say that again. I'd like to have your job.'

'It's not so bad.' Anders tried not to look smug. 'But you have to know how to handle them. Think you'll catch this nut?'

'Me?' McNeil shook his head. 'Nothing to do with me. I've got beyond catching anyone. I'm like you ... taking it easy, but the Chief will catch him. Terrell's got a head on his shoulders, but, of course it'll take time.'

A gleaming sand coloured Rolls drew up and leaving McNeil, Anders stepped briskly across the red carpet and opened the car door.

'Morning, Jack.' The handsome fat man who got out of the Rolls was Rodney Branzenstein. He was a successful Corporation lawyer who came every morning to see clients living at the hotel. 'Seen anything of Mrs. Dunc Browler?'

'Too early for her, sir,' Anders said. 'In about fifteen minutes.'

'If she asks you, tell her I haven't arrived.' Branzenstein slid a dollar bill into Anders' ready hand. He strode into the hotel.

While his chauffeur drove the Rolls away, McNeil moved close to Anders.

'Do you ever get sore fingers, Jack?' he asked with concern.

'Not me,' Anders said promptly, 'but don't get wrong ideas. This has taken years.'

'Is that right?' McNeil shook his head. 'I've been pounding this goddam beat for years and no one has ever thought to slip me a buck.'

'My personality,' Anders said. 'Your bad luck.'

A tiny woman with sky blue hair, her skin raddled, her aged fingers crooked by diamond rings came tottering out of the hotel.

Anders was immediately by her side.

'Mrs. Clayton!' Watching him, McNeil was startled by the look of incredulity on Anders' red, leathery face. 'Now where do you think you're going?'

The little woman simpered and looked adoringly up at Anders.

'I thought I'd go for a very short walk.'

'Mrs. Clayton!' The concern in Anders' voice made even Mc-Neil concerned. 'Did Dr. Lowenstein say you could go for a very short walk?'

The little woman looked guilty.

'To be honest, Anders, he didn't.'

'I should think not!' Anders took her elbow gently and began to guide her back into the hotel. 'You sit quietly, Mrs. Clayton. I'll get Mr. Bevan to call Dr. Lowenstein. I can't have you running around wild, now can I?'

'Sweet Jesus!' McNeil muttered and was so impressed, he crossed himself.

Some minutes later, Anders came back and rested his corns on the red carpet. McNeil was still there, breathing heavily, his small Irish eyes glassy.

'That was Mrs. Henry William Clayton,' Anders told him. 'Her old man kicked off five years ago. He left her five million bucks.'

McNeil's eyes opened wide.

'You mean that old bag of bones is worth five million bucks?'

Anders frowned at him.

'Pat! You shouldn't speak disrespectfully of the dead.'

'Yeah.' There was a long pause, then McNeil said, 'You sort of shoved her around, didn't you?'

'That's the way to handle them. She loves it. She knows I'm the only one who cares about her.'

'Have you got any more like her in this joint?' McNeil asked.

'The hotel is stuffed with them.' Anders shook his head. 'Dotty old people with too much money . . . it's sad.'

'It wouldn't make me sad,' McNeil said. 'Well, I guess I'll leave you to it. See you.' He paused, then regarded Anders. 'How much did she slip you?'

Anders lowered his right eyelid in a heavy wink.

'That's a trade secret, Paddy.'

'Man! Am I in the wrong trade!' Sighing, McNeil started down the boulevard, his big feet slapping on the sidewalk.

Lying on the flat roof of the Pelota night club, Poke Toholo watched the big police officer depart. He watched him through the telescopic sight of the target rifle.

Poke had been on the roof now for the past three hours. The four storey building was a little under a thousand yards from the Plaza Beach hotel. Poke had arrived there in the Buick at

06.00, a time when he could be sure there would be no one around to see him leave the car and carrying the rifle.

He was familiar with the Club: one of the oldest buildings in the City. It had a swing down iron fire escape at the rear which was considered by tourists to be a novelty and something to gape at. The climb to the roof had been made without danger or difficulty, but Poke, as he lay concealed by the low wall surrounding the roof, knew that getting down to the street again would be much more dangerous. The boulevard by then would be busy, the adjacent buildings alive with people and he risked being seen, but he was prepared to take the risk.

He looked at his wristwatch. The time now was 09.43. He again applied his eye to the telescopic sight and began to search the boulevard.

Traffic was building up. People were appearing, moving in a steady stream up and down the boulevard. Then he saw Chuck and he nodded his approval. Chuck was on time: a little early, but that didn't matter. Chuck, wearing a clean red and white check shirt and grey hipsters, looked like any other of the young tourists who swarmed into the City at this season. He was idling along, reading a newspaper.

Poke slightly adjusted the screw of the telescopic sight, bringing Chuck's face into sharp focus. He saw he was sweating. That was understandable. Chuck had a tricky job to do: quite as dangerous as what Poke had to do.

Again Poke looked at his watch. Only another few minutes, he thought and shifted the telescopic sight to the entrance to the Plaza Beach hotel. Focusing the cross hairs on Anders' head, he satisfied himself that it would be a certain shot.

Oblivious to what was going on, Anders surveyed the boulevard, nodded to those who nodded to him, touched his peak cap to those who merited a salute and basked in the warmth of the sun.

Since the coming of the mini skirt, the bare midriff and the see-through dress, Anders' life had become much more interesting. With approval, he watched the girls prance by. As a doorman, he relied for a living on the old, the fat and the rich, but that didn't mean he had lost his appreciation for long legs, a twitching bottom or a bouncy breast.

Then Mrs. Dunc Browler appeared.

Anders was expecting her. Invariably at this hour she made her appearance. He gave her his best salute, his smile bright, kindly and friendly: a smile he only switched on for his special people.

Mrs. Dunc Browler was a short, stout woman in her late sixties. Perhaps the word 'stout' was an understatement. By eating five large meals a day for most of her sixty-seven years she had managed to cover her small frame with a layer of fat that would make an elephant anxious. She was one of the many eccentrics who lived permanently in the hotel. It went without saying that she was rich: just how rich no one knew, but the fact that she had one of the best suites in the hotel that cost $300 a day for the suite alone pointed to the fact that she was pretty well heeled.

Since losing her husband who she had doted on some four years ago, she had bought a large floppy bitch from the dog pound for something like three dollars and Anders considered she had been conned. Admittedly the dog was affectionate but to Anders' snobbish eyes, she had no class.

'That dog's mother should have been ashamed of herself,' he had said while discussing the dog with the assistant doorman.

But to Mrs. Dunc Browler, Lucy, as the dog was called was her child, her dearest possession, her friend, her companion and Anders, knowing people's weaknesses, accepted the fact.

So when Mrs. Dunc Browler made her appearance, wearing flowing white robes that would have delighted a P. & G. account executive and a huge hat covered with artificial cherries, apricots and lemons to take Lucy for her constitutional, Anders went into his act.

'Good morning, ma'am,' he said with a bow, 'and how is Miss Lucy this morning, ma'am?'

Mrs. Dunc Browler beamed with pleasure. She thought Anders was a dear man, so kind and his interest in Lucy filled her heart with pleasure.

'She's fine,' she said. 'Absolutely fine.' Directing her beaming smile down to the panting dog, she went on, 'Say good morning to nice Anders, Lucy, dear.'

The dog regarded Anders with overfed bored eyes, then squatting, she made a small puddle on the red carpet.

'Oh dear.' Mrs. Dunc Browler looked helplessly at Anders. 'I should have brought my darling down a little earlier ... quite my fault.'

The carpet would have to be removed, cleaned and another

installed, but this was no skin off Anders' nose. As the old girl paid $300 a day to stay at the hotel, why should he worry?

'Little accidents will happen ma'am,' he said. 'You have a fine morning for a walk.'

'Yes . . . a lovely morning. While Lucy was having her breakfast, I was listening to the birds. They . . .'

Those were the last words Mrs. Dunc Browler was to utter.

The bullet smashed through her ridiculous hat and into her brain. She sank to the red carpet like a stricken elephant.

For a split second Anders looked down at the dead woman at his feet, then his Army trained mind took over. He had seen so many men shot through the head by snipers in the past that he immediately realised what had happened. He whirled around, his keen eyes searching the distant roof tops. While women screamed, men shouted and pushed forward, while cars came to a grinding halt, Anders caught a glimpse of a man ducking out of sight behind a low wall surrounding the roof of the Pelota nightclub.

Anders was wasted no time pointing and shouting. Ploughing his way through the gathering crowd, he lumbered into the road and started off towards the nightclub at the end of the boulevard.

'Jack!'

Without stopping, Anders looked over his shoulder. He saw Police Officer McNeil pounding up behind him.

'The bastard's up there!' Anders panted and pointed to the roof of the nightclub. 'Come on, Paddy! We'll get him!'

But age, soft living and too many shots of Cutty Sark were already taking toll of Anders' legs. His stride began to falter as McNeil reached him.

'I saw him!' Anders gasped. 'The fire escape, Paddy!'

McNeil grunted and pounded past Anders, his big hand snatching his gun from its holster. People gaped at him and moved hurriedly out of his way. None of them went with him to help. This was strictly police business: why should they stick their necks out?

As Poke Toholo came slithering down the fire escape, McNeil came charging around the building. They saw each other at the same time. McNeil saw the Indian had a gun in his hand. He pulled up, his barrel shaped chest heaving from his run, and swung up his gun arm. As his finger tightened on the trigger, he felt a violent blow in his chest that lifted him off his feet and sent him crashing down on his back.

Poke took the last ten steps of the escape in a jump and made for the parking lot. McNeil forced himself up, lifted his gun as Poke looked back over his shoulder. Seeing the gun aiming at him, Poke swerved aside as McNeil fired, then paused to take careful aim, he shot McNeil through the head. Spinning around, he raced into the parking lot, his black eyes looking for danger. Only a dozen or so cars, left over night, greeted his eyes. It took but a moment to find one of them unlocked. He slid into the back seat, shut the door and crouched down.

He was out of sight as Anders, panting, his face purple from his exertions, came into the parking lot and found McNeil's body.

One brief look told Anders that McNeil was beyond his help. He snatched up McNeil's gun and started across the parking lot to the far exit, sure his man had gone that way. As he did so three frightened faced men came reluctantly into the parking lot. Seeing Anders with a gun in his hand and recognising him by his uniform as the doorman of the Plaza Beach hotel, they plucked up their courage and ran after him.

Unflustered, Poke watched them go, then taking out his handkerchief, he carefully wiped the gun. He would have to leave it, he thought regretfully. He lifted the car seat and thrust the gun out of sight.

More people were spilling into the car park. Police and ambulance sirens were making the air hideous with noise. Sliding out of the car, moving unhurriedly, Poke walked over to the crowd surrounding the dead policeman. The crowd accepted him as one of themselves. He was still standing gaping as they were gaping when the car park became flooded with policemen. He allowed himself to be herded away with the others and when he reached the main boulevard, he moved slowly and quietly back to the Buick.

While all this was going on, Chuck, sweat running down his face, had joined the milling crowd surrounding Mrs. Dunc Browler's body. No one had eyes for her dog, Lucy who stood on the edge of the kerb in fat bewilderment. Chuck bent over the dog, his hand going to her collar. Lucy disliked strangers. She backed away. Cursing, Chuck grabbed her. No one noticed him.

It was only after the police had restored order, after some of the hotel staff had rushed out to cover Mrs. Dunc Browler's body with a sheet and after the crowd had been dispersed that the assistant manager of the hotel, a dog lover himself, remembered Lucy. It was he who found the luggage tag fastened to Lucy's collar. Written on the tab in printed letters was the legend:

The Executioner.

Four

The news that a killer was loose in a City more famous for its idle rich than Monte Carlo made banner headlines in the press of the world. Foreign newsmen and independent TV units and the like descended on the City like a flock of vultures. They invaded every hotel and motel and were even prepared to take to tents when room accommodation ran out.

The man they were after was Doorman Jack Anders, being the only one to have caught a glimpse of the Executioner, but before they could get at him, he had been whisked from the scene. After a brief consultation with the Director of the Plaza Beach hotel, Mayor Hedley had persuaded him that Anders would be better off for a while with his brother who lived in Dallas. Anders had been smart enough to accept the situation. The old, the rich and the raddled would not take kindly to him once he became a TV character. Limelight was their prerogative and not the prerogative of a hotel doorman.

Before he was smuggled out of the City, Anders had been interrogated by Beigler with Terrell and Hedley sitting in.

Beigler knew he was dealing with an old soldier: a man with a keen mind and whose observation could be trusted. He knew Anders wouldn't exaggerate to make himself important as so many people in his place could have done. He was sure the facts Anders gave him were facts he could rely on.

'Don't rush this, Jack,' Beigler said. 'Let's go over it again.' He looked at the notes he had taken. 'Mrs. Browler always left the hotel at 9.45 . . . right?'

56

Anders nodded.

'This was a set routine?'

Again Anders nodded.

'This routine . . . how long has it been going on?'

'Since she has been with us . . . some five years.'

'Mrs. Browler was a well-known character. You could say she was an eccentric . . . right?'

'She was that all right.'

'So a lot of people would know she would leave the hotel at this time.'

'Yes.'

'Okay, Jack. We have this established. Let's skip to the shooting. You were talking to her: then it happened. Let's go over that again.'

'Like I said: I saw by the head wound and by the way she fell she had been shot by a high velocity rifle,' Anders said. I looked around. There were one or two possible places for a sniper to be hidden, but the best place was the roof of the Pelota club. I looked that way and I saw the killer.'

'Now let's take this slowly,' Beigler said. 'You've already told us you caught a glimpse of the killer. Let's try to develop this. I'm not asking you for facts this time. I'm asking you for an impression. You get me? Don't worry about whether the impression is right or wrong. Just give me your impression.'

Anders thought for a moment.

'I saw a movement. I didn't see a man . . . it was a movement. By this movement, I knew a man was up there. I knew this man, by the way he ducked out of sight, was the sniper . . . so I went after him.'

'That's not what I asked you,' Beigler said patiently. 'You've already told me that. You saw a movement and you knew there was a man up there. Okay, now I'm asking you for an impression of this man.'

Anders looked uneasily at Terrell and Hedley, then he looked back at Beigler.

'I'm giving you the facts,' he said.

'I have your facts here.' Beigler tapped his notebook. 'Now I want you to sound off. You had a glimpse of a man ducking behind the wall. Was he white or coloured? Don't think about it . . . just give me your impression. I don't give a damn if you're right or wrong. Was he white or coloured?'

'Coloured.' Then Anders caught himself up and shook his

57

head. 'I don't know why I said that. I don't know. I just saw a movement. I tell you I didn't see him.'

'But you have the impression he was coloured?'

'I don't know. Yes . . . maybe. He could have been sun tanned. I can't swear to it. I did get the idea he was dark.'

'What was he wearing?'

Anders began to look worried.

'How do I know? I told you . . .'

'Was he wearing a black shirt, a white shirt, or a coloured shirt?'

'Maybe a coloured shirt.' Anders rubbed his sweating chin. 'I'm trying to help, but I don't want you to talk me into telling you lies.'

Beigler looked at Terrell who nodded.

'Okay, Jack, thanks,' he said. 'You've been a help,' and the session was over.

When Anders had gone, Hedley said, 'You call that helpful? You practically talked him into giving false evidence!'

'Anders has a trained mind,' Terrell said quietly. 'He has an impressive record as a combat soldier. I'd rather go along with an impression from him than so called solid evidence from the usual witnesses we get. Anders has been helpful.'

Hedley shrugged and got to his feet.

'Three killings! And what have we got? Nothing!'

'You may not think so, but I do,' Terrell said. 'You see, Lawson, you don't understand police work. Right now we have one concrete and one abstract clue. We now know this man isn't working alone. Someone let the air out of Riddle's tyre so the killer would find Lisa Mendoza alone. Someone clipped a luggage tag on Mrs. Browler's dog . . . so we know this man has help. We now have a hint that this man could be coloured. You say we have nothing, but I don't.'

'But what does it amount to?' Hedley asked. 'This lunatic . . .'

'Take it easy, Lawson. Come with me.' Terrell got up and putting his hand on Hedley's arm, he led him down the passage and into the Detectives' room. Every desk was occupied. Each detective was talking to a witness who had either seen Mrs. Dunc Browler shot or had heard about McCuen's murder or knew something about Riddle and his mistress: eager, public spirited people, longing to give information, most of it worthless, but some of it that just might steer the police closer to the

Executioner. The queue of these people extended along the corridor, down the stairs and to the street. 'One or more of these people,' Terrell said, 'could come up with a clue. This is police work, Lawson. Sooner or later we will get him.'

'And in the meantime he could kill again.'

'Sooner or later he will make a mistake . . . they all do.'

'So what do I tell the press?'

'That we are continuing the investigation. Don't tell them anything else,' Terrell said. 'This is important . . . if you have to blame someone, blame me. Say we are doing our best.'

Hedley nodded, then went down the stairs past the long queue of sweating, patient people and on to the waiting press men.

Terrell returned to his office where Beigler was waiting. The two men looked at each other.

'Well, now he's gone, let's see what we have so far,' Terrell said and sat down. He reached for a sheet of paper on which he had made notes, broken down from the summaries of reports supplied by his men. 'We could just be getting a picture: not much of a picture, but maybe something. I'm still after the motive. These three victims were all top class bridge players and members of the Fifty Club.' He looked up from his notes. 'What do we know about the Fifty Club?'

Beigler knew Paradise City far better than Terrell did and Terrell knew it. He had only to ask Beigler any question about the City and Beigler never failed to come up with an accurate answer.

'The Fifty Club? Super snob . . . hand picked members. The entrance fee is around $15,000 and the sub twice that. If you get elected, you can consider yourself one of the top snobs of the City, but you have to play bridge at professional standards.'

'Well, McCuen, Riddle and Mrs. Browler were members . . . could mean something . . . could mean nothing. We'll have to talk to someone at the club. The motive could just possibly be there. Another thing that interests me is the killer is familiar with the way the victims lived. He knew Mrs. Browler left her hotel at 9.45. He knew McCuen always left his house at three minutes after nine and he knew Lisa Mendoza would be at the bungalow on a Friday night. This makes a pattern. This man is local.'

Beigler nodded.

'So we start looking for a man who has this inside information. Maybe a servant at the Club. I'll get men onto these people who Riddle mentioned before he knocked himself off.'

Terrell reached for his pipe.

'Do you think he could be coloured, Joe?'

'Your guess is as good as mine, but Anders seemed to think so.'

The telephone bell rang. Terrell scooped up the receiver, listened, grunted, said, 'Okay ... thanks ... yes, get the report over to me,' and he hung up. 'That was Melville.' They've checked out the rifle. It killed McCuen and Mrs. Browler, but of course there are no prints. Danvaz has identified it. That doesn't get us far.'

'Except this bastard now hasn't a rifle,' Beigler pointed out.

'That won't stop him stealing another, will it?' Terrell said and set fire to his pipe.

*

If there was one thing Lepski hated among a lot of things he hated it was interviewing people and writing reports. He thought anyone who offered themselves voluntarily to be questioned should be in a home for the mental retarded. But he accepted the fact that this was police work. When he could avoid it, he avoided it, but when he was stuck with it as he was now stuck with it, he handled the situation and somehow managed to restrain his temper. He was now looking with despair at the ever lengthening line of people, eagerly waiting to be questioned.

Max Jacoby was at the next desk. He had just got through coping with a voluble old man who had seen Mrs. Dunc Browler die. All the old man could talk about was the artificial fruit on her hat. He was trying to convince Jacoby that the killer had been hostile to the fruit on her hat. Jacoby finally got rid of him as Lepski finally got rid of an old lady who was explaining to him that Mrs. Dunc Browler's lovely dog had seen the killer and shouldn't the police do something about it?

The two men looked at each other.

'How's life?' Jacoby asked with a tired grin.

Very aware he was Jacoby's senior, Lepski glowered at him.

'This is police work,' he said. 'You have to dig deep to find water.'

Jacoby shook his head in mock wonderment.

'Is that what we're looking for?'

A fat, elderly, shabbily dressed man sat down with a thud

before Jacoby's desk and with a suppressed groan Jacoby reached for another pad of paper.

'Yes, sir? Your name and address?'

Morons! Lepski thought. Three goddamn hours and nothing! Stupid hunk-heads having the afternoon off! He spiked his last report and as he reached for a cigarette, a cloud of perfume drifted over him. Looking up, he found a girl had slid into the chair opposite his desk and was looking at him, wide eyed and concerned.

'You look hot and tired, you poor dear,' she said.

Lepski's loins quivered. This was the kind of doll you saw only in the pages of *Playboy*. A dolly bird who could resurrect a male corpse: a gorgeously built blonde with large violet coloured eyes and eyelashes that would shame a cow. Her mammary equipment made Lepski's breath hiss between his teeth. He became aware that Jacoby, the fat, elderly man, four detectives, borrowed from Miami police headquarters and three patrolmen who were keeping the line of waiting witnesses in order, were all gaping at the girl.

Lepski glared around the room and the rest of his colleagues reluctantly got back to work.

'Yes?' he barked in his cop voice. It was a voice that usually had a devastating impact on most people but it made no impression on this girl. She lifted one heavy breast to settle it more comfortably in its bra cradle, touched a straying curl in her silky blonde hair and repeated, 'You look hot and tired.'

Lepski made a small noise like a fly trapped in an envelope.

The fat, elderly man who had a face like a Dutch cheese leaned forward and breathed garlic fumes into Lepski's face. 'Excuse me, mister,' he said, beaming, 'the little lady's right ... that's what you look ... hot and tired.'

Lepski scrumpled a sheet of paper.

'Will you take care of your witness?' he snarled at Jacoby. The venom in his voice made the fat, elderly man wilt. Then Lepski turned his attention to the girl.

'You want to say something?'

The girl was regarding him with admiring eyes.

'Gee! I heard tales about the cops here, but I didn't know they could be anything like you ... honest.'

Lepski put his tie straight.

'Look, miss, we're busy here,' he said in a softer tone. Her genuine admiration had made an impact. 'Just what is it?'

61

'The girls told me I should come.'

Lepski sighed and reached for a fresh sheet of paper.

'Name and address, please?'

'I'm Mandy Lucas. I work and live at the club.'

'What club?'

'You know ... the Pelota Club.'

'You live there?'

She wrinkled her pretty nose.

'I have a room there ... you can't call it living.'

'You have information, Miss Lucas?'

'Well, the girls said I should come, but I don't know ... it's a bit smelly in here, isn't it? All these people ... but meeting you! Gee! When I tell the girls about you, they'll have off their pants!'

Lepski's eyes bulged. He glanced at Jacoby who was listening, his eyes also bulging and then at the fat, elderly man who was goggling.

Recalling that he was 1st Grade now, Lepski leaned forward and screwed his face into his cop scowl.

'Look, Miss Lucas, what have you to tell me?'

The girl, arranged her other breast more comfortably as she said, 'Call me Mandy ... none of my real friends ever call me Miss Lucas.'

'Okay, Mandy ...' Lepski crossed his leg, shifted a ball pen from right to left with some violence and from somewhere inside him came a noise like a fall of stones. 'Now tell me why you're here.'

'You really want to know? I told the girls I'd be just wasting your time ... honest.' Her long eyelashes fluttered. 'I know how you boys here must be working like stinko. But the girls ... well, they said ...'

'Yeah.' Lepski was getting concerned about his blood pressure. 'It's my job. Never mind about wasting my goldamn ... I mean my time ... just tell me.'

'Gee! It's hot in here!' She stood up, wriggled, lifted her mini skirt slightly away from her body, then sat down. 'Are you a married man, Mr. Detective?'

'I'm married,' Lepski said in a resigned voice.

She leaned forward and whispered confidentially, 'Then you'll understand. These goddamn disposable panties are hell.'

Lepski's eyes nearly fell out of their sockets.

'Does your wife ever complain?' the girl asked.

In a strangled voice, Lepski said, 'Mandy! Will you tell me why you're here!'

'Oh, gee! I'm sorry. You mustn't mind me. I'm scatty. You really want to know . . . no kidding?'

'Just go right ahead,' Lepski said in a voice that would have surprised a Mina bird.

'Well, I saw this guy. He really was a sexy thing.' She leaned forward and the front of her dress sagged so Lepski caught a glimpse of her nipples. 'I don't dig for darkies. I don't want you to imagine I have anything against non-whites. You understand? But usually I don't dig for them. But there are times . . . I mean a man is a man and this man was a real doll!'

Lepski made a noise like a disturbed bee-hive.

'Just when did you see this man, Mandy?'

'Right after this horrible shooting. It woke me up . . . the shooting, I mean. I heard all this yelling.' She hitched up her bra strap. 'When I wake up, I'm practically dead. Do you wake up like that? You know . . . dead . . . eyes gummy . . . head reeling?'

Lepski's fingers turned into hooks.

'You saw this man in the parking lot?'

'Well, there were people jumping around . . . you know something?'

'Keep going.'

'Well, these people reminded me of those Mexican beans . . . you know . . . the things that jump around . . . kids like them.'

Lepski made a noise like a circular saw hitting a knot of wood.

Mandy stared at him.

'When you make a noise like that, my mother told me you should say "pardon".'

Lepski looked down at his blotter, held onto himself then after a pause, he said, 'So okay, the people were jumping around like Mexican beans. What happened then?'

'This poor cop . . . I mean police officer . . . lying there. It turned me right over. Imagine! My eyes nearly fell out! Then I saw this doll get out of the car!'

Lepski leaned back in his chair. He hummed a few bars of the National Anthem under his breath to try to calm himself.

'You saw a man get out of a parked car in the parking lot?'

Her eyes opened wide.

'I said that, didn't I? Or did I say something else? Honest, I sometimes don't know what I do say.' She lifted herself off her chair, made adjusting movements to her skirt, watched with interest by everyone in the room, and sat down again. 'I don't suppose you ever get that way. I mean saying something and forgetting right after what you've said. You wouldn't have to worry about a thing like that, would you?'

Lepski loosened his tie.

'No.'

'Well, I do. It makes my life miserable.'

'You were saying: you saw a man get out of a car parked in the parking lot. Is this what you have to tell me?'

'That's what the girls told me I must tell you.' She suppressed a nervous giggle. 'Honest, I'm sorry. I just knew I would be wasting your time, but the girls . . .'

'No one wastes my time. I'm here to receive information,' Lepski said. He wrote fast on a sheet of paper, then shoved the paper over to the girl. 'This says you saw a coloured man get out of a car in the parking lot where Police Officer McNeil was shot. Right?'

She peered short-sightedly at what he had written, then she nodded.

'I guess that's right, but shouldn't you say that it's my car and the battery's flat and I haven't used it in weeks?'

Sweat broke out on Lepski's face. He realised because he was so bored with the people who were offering him worthless information he had been on the verge of missing an important clue.

'Would you say that again?'

Mandy repeated what she had said.

'That's why the girls told me to come down here, but I said you'd think I was crazy.'

'I don't think you're crazy,' Lepski said. 'Just tell me exactly what you saw.'

Her eyes opened wide.

'But I've already told you.'

'I want to hear it all over again.'

'My goodness! Do you think it's important?'

'It could be,' Lepski said, mopping his face with his handkerchief. 'It could be.'

*

Two hours later, Chief of Police Terrell arrived at Mayor Hedley's office.

Hedley looking white and strained had just come off the telephone. For the past three hours he had been coping with non-stop and hysterical demands from his rich friends for police protection. Their selfish insistence for personal protection had infuriated him and when he saw Terrell he drew in a breath of relief.

'Goddamn it! Do you realise a lot of people are actually leaving the City . . . like refugees!'

'Should we care about them?' Terrell asked as he sat down.

'This is a hell of a thing! What do you mean . . . of course we've got to care!'

'We've got our first break.'

Hedley stared at him, then leaned forward eagerly.

'Break? What break?'

'We now have a description of the killer. I told you sooner or later if we kept digging something would turn up, but I didn't expect we'd get this break so fast.'

'Well, for God's sake! Tell me!'

'The Pelota Club employs six girls as hostesses,' Terrell said, settling himself more comfortably in his chair. 'They have rooms on the top floor of the club: rooms that overlook the car park where McNeil was gunned down. One of these girls . . . Mandy Lucas . . . owns a Ford car which she hasn't used in weeks and it's left in this parking lot. The noise of the shooting woke her. Looking out of her window she saw the crowd milling around McNeil's body, then she claims to have seen a man getting out of her car and join the crowd. We now have the car in the police yard. Under the rear seat we've found the gun that killed McNeil. This man, Mandy saw, must have hidden in the car to avoid Anders, then when Anders went on and a crowd began to swarm around McNeil's body, this man hid his gun under the rear seat, left the car and mingled with the crowd. He's a man with a lot of nerve, but what he didn't allow for was someone like Mandy Lucas being at a window to see him.'

'Well, for God's sake!' Hedley sat back. 'This woman give you a description?'

'Yes. She's pretty dumb but she claims she would know him anywhere. A claim like that is always doubtful. Too often we've had witnesses who swear they can pick out a man but fail when we set up a parade. But she says the man is an Indian and that jells with Anders' impression. According to her, he is around twenty-five years of age, thick black hair, well built and an Indian. She stresses this ... he isn't a negro, but an Indian and he was wearing a yellow and white flowered pattern shirt and dark blue hipsters.'

Hedley slapped his hand down on his desk.

'This is really something at last! Did you get his prints from the gun?'

'No. He knows what he is doing. He doesn't leave prints.'

'Have you given the description to the press?'

'No.' Terrell regarded Hedley. 'We'll have to, of course, but I thought I'd better talk to you first. I don't have to remind you we have over a hundred Seminole Indians working in various jobs in this City. The bulk of them are young: most of them wear flowered pattern shirts and hipsters ... it's a uniform. To most people an Indian looks like any other Indian. This description helps us, but it could cause trouble.'

'Yes.' Hedley thought, frowning. 'I see what you're getting at, but we have no alternative, Frank. You and this office are being criticised for not coming up with anything. I'll call a press conference right away. This is news we can't sit on.'

Terrell nodded.

'My men are out already, concentrating on the Indian district. This man is local. I'm sure of that.' He got to his feet. 'I wish the girl had said he was a white man.'

'Well, at least we have something,' Hedley said and reached for his telephone.

As Terrell left, he heard Hedley calling for his Press officer.

*

Meg lay on the bed and watched the blue-bottle fly walk across the ceiling. Her watch told her it was around midday. It could be later. Her watch usually lost ten minutes in the hour and if she didn't remember to push it on, after a while, its hands didn't make sense, but she didn't care.

She was not only bored, but worried.

Chuck had gone out while she had been sleeping and now there was still no sign of him. She couldn't be bothered to get off the bed to get herself a cup of coffee. She wanted a cup of coffee, but the effort involved was too much for her. It was so much easier to lie there watching the fly than to do anything else.

66

After a while, the fly flew away and she envied it. That's what she would like to be able to do: fly away. It must be marvellous, she thought, just to take off, to have no thoughts, to drop on a bit of meat for food, then to fly away again . . . lucky fly!

She shut her eyes and slid into a doze. That was one thing she could do without effort. That was the only thing she was any good at, she thought.

She woke to find the fly back on the ceiling. She felt uncomfortably hot and sticky. Languidly, she looked at her watch. The time according to the watch was 14.35. It couldn't be as late as that, she thought, watching the fly as it walked around the ceiling. Marvellous to be able to do that, she thought. I'd like to do it . . . just walk around on the ceiling, upside down. Then sudden cold fear gripped her. Where was Chuck? She sat up and threw off the sheet. He had been gone for hours! Had he walked out on her?

With a flurry, she was off the bed and to the window and opened it. She peered out, looking across at the hut that served as the Motel's office. She caught sight of Mrs. Bertha Harris moving about. There were no cars in the parking lot. Where was Chuck? Again she looked at her watch. It couldn't be so late! She held the watch to her ear. The damn thing had stopped! It could be even later! In panic, she scrambled into her stretch pants, dragged a dirty sweater over her head, thrust her feet into sandals and started for the door. As she passed the small wall mirror, she caught sight of herself and she paused.

God! She looked a mess!

She darted into the shower room and threw water on her face. Then drying her face, she dragged a comb through her long, tangled hair. As she came out of the shower room, she saw Chuck standing in the open doorway.

'Where have you been?' she demanded shrilly. 'I've been waiting and waiting . . . where have you been?'

Chuck closed the door. There was a set expression on his face that frightened her.

'Pack up!' he said curtly. 'We're leaving.'

He went to the closet, grabbed his few belongings and threw them on the bed.

'Where are we going?'

He caught hold of her arm, spun her around and slapped her buttocks with a viciousness that made her squeal.

'Get packed!'

She backed away, staring at him.

'Want more?' he asked, moving forward threateningly.

'No!'

She hurriedly pulled her rucksack from under the bed, then going to the chest of drawers, she began throwing her things on the bed beside his.

The cabin door opened and Poke Toholo looked in.

'Chuck.' He beckoned and then backed away.

'Pack my things,' Chuck said. 'We take off in five minutes,' and he went out and into Poke's cabin.

Poke had his rucksack packed.

'Yeah.'

'Is she all right?' he asked.

Chuck nodded.

'You know where to go and what to do?'

'Yeah.'

'See if the old woman wants more money. Be careful how you handle her.'

'We've been over that,' Chuck said impatiently.

'So long as you remember.' Poke picked up his rucksack. 'I'll get off. Don't forget: ten o'clock any morning.'

'I'll be waiting.'

Poke slung the rucksack on his back.

'The last one didn't go so well,' he said as if talking to himself, 'but it was tricky.' He looked at Chuck, his black eyes glittering. 'That cop asked for it.'

Chuck didn't say anything.

'The cops hate a cop killer.' Poke eased the straps of his rucksack. 'That means they hate you as much as me – if they find us.'

Chuck's eyes narrowed.

'Do you think you have to scare me?' he asked.

Poke regarded him.

'I just want you to remember . . . she's in it too.'

'Okay . . . I'm not deaf.'

'You'll be hearing from me.' Poke went past Chuck and into the sunshine.

Chuck watched him stride away. When he had lost sight of him, he went over to the motel's office.

Mrs. Harris was eating a hamburger which she held in a paper napkin.

'We're checking out, ma'am,' Chuck said.

Mrs. Harris's four chins became two as she lifted her head.

'You said you were staying longer.'

Chuck had his tale prepared.

'We ran into friends. They want us to stay with them. We paid for a week, didn't we? Do you owe us something or do we owe you something?'

Mrs. Harris took another bite out of the hamburger and munched while she regarded her account book.

'No, I guess we're quits,' she said. 'You have still two days to go, but you didn't give me notice. Let's call it quits.'

'Okay, ma'am.' Chuck put a dollar bill on the counter. 'That's for the old man. Thanks, ma'am. We've been comfortable. Maybe if we're this way again, we'll look in.'

Mrs. Harris beamed.

'You'll always be welcomed.' She whipped up the dollar bill. 'The Indian going as well?'

'Oh sure . . . we're all going.'

Mrs. Harris chased a piece of onion off her lips with her tongue.

'Is he a friend of yours?'

Chuck had been well coached. He shook his head.

'He's just a nice guy my wife and I ran into on the road. He's going to Key West now . . . got a job waiting for him.' He smiled. 'Well, we'll get on. So long, ma'am.'

He returned to the cabin where Meg was waiting with the two rucksacks packed.

'Let's go,' Chuck said, picking up the rucksacks.

'Where are we going?'

He turned and glared at her.

'Will you never learn to keep your goddamn mouth shut?' he snarled.

'Can't I say anything?' Meg said with a flash of spirit. 'Can't I even ask where we're going?'

'Oh, come on!'

Chuck carried the rucksacks to the Buick, dumped them on the back seat and slid under the wheel. Meg got in beside him.

'Where's Poke?' she asked. 'Don't we wait for him?'

Chuck stared at her and this time the expression in his eyes chilled her.

'Who's Poke? What are you talking about?' he said and started the engine.

She began to speak, then stopped.

'That's it.' Chuck shifted into drive. 'That's more like it.'

The car moved forward and he drove away from the motel and onto the highway, leading to Paradise City.

When they reached the City, he avoided the main boulevards, cutting down the side streets until he reached the harbour. He found parking space on the waterfront, cut the engine and slid out of the car.

'Come on,' he said, dragging his rucksack out of the car. 'Get yours. We walk now.'

Together, their rucksacks bowing them down, they walked along the waterfront that teemed with activity. This was the commercial end of the harbour with its sponge boats and its turtle crawls.

Walking blindly, Meg followed Chuck who seemed to know where he was going.

They trudged past a rattlesnake cannery. Above the factory was a red neon sign picturing a coiled snake. Another sign, blinking on and off read: *Snake Snaks*. They made their way through the milling crowd and around the fruit market, then Chuck led the way down a smelly alley, lined either side by two storey, weather beaten wooden buildings. He stopped outside the end building and dropped his rucksack.

'Stick around,' he said and went through the doorway, protected against the flies by multi-coloured nylon strips.

At the end of a short, dark corridor, a fat Seminole Indian sat behind a desk, gnawing at a chicken leg.

Chuck said, 'We're booked in here . . . Mr. and Mrs. Jones.'

The Indian dropped the chicken bone out of sight, slightly raised himself to wipe his fingers clean on the seat of his trousers, then settled back in his chair. He smiled, revealing a mouthful of gold capped teeth.

'The room's all ready, Mr. Jones. First floor, left. No. 3.'

'I'll get my wife,' Chuck said.

The Indian continued to beam.

'That's it, Mr. Jones, you get your wife.'

It was a back room, overlooking the harbour. There was a double bed, a rickety chest of drawers, a wall closet and surprisingly, a telephone that stood on the night table by the bed. The so-called bathroom and the smelly toilet were across the landing.

Meg dropped her rucksack on the floor and looked around the room.

'Why couldn't we have stayed at the motel instead of moving into this awful dump?' she asked, and with a hopeless gesture, she slumped on the bed.

Chuck went to the window and looked down at the waterfront. He stood there for some minutes, fascinated by the noise and the activity, then he turned and came over to the bed.

Meg looked up at him.

'Honest, Chuck, there are times when I think you're crazy,' she said. 'Why leave the motel? It was comfortable. Why come to this awful dump?'

He stared at her, his eyes like glass.

'What motel?'

Meg shivered. She pressed her hands to her face.

'Chuck! What is this? Are you trying to drive me nuts? I ask you about Poke and you say who is Poke. Now I ... you say what motel! What is it? What's the matter with you ... or is it me?'

'There's nothing the matter with me, baby,' Chuck said quietly. 'We never met Poke. We never stayed at a motel.'

Meg lifted her tangled hair in a gesture of despair.

'You mean that's what I tell the police?'

Chuck grinned.

'Now, baby, you're showing you do have brains. That's it. No Poke ... no motel.'

Suddenly her dreary, nagging parents, her dreary home came into her mind as a haven of refuge.

'No, Chuck.' She hurt herself by beating her clenched fists against her forehead. 'No! I'm going! You carry on with that crazy Indian! I don't want to know anything ... I won't say anything. I'm going!'

'Are you?'

The tone in his voice made her stiffen.

Chuck had taken out his flick knife. The gleaming blade made her shrink back.

'You're in, baby,' he said gently. 'I warned you and you said you were in. You quit now and I'll slice you. You want to go through the rest of your life with your face hacked up?'

She stared at the knife in horror. Chuck watched her, then grinned. He put the knife back in his pocket.

'Come on, baby, let's go look at the town.'

She sat motionless, her arms folded tightly around her stomach.

'It's there . . . just across the way,' Chuck said.

He watched her scramble across the corridor, then when the toilet flushed, he left the bedroom, closed the door and locked it. He was waiting for her at the head of the stairs.

Side by side, they went down the stairs, past the fat smiling Indian and into the noisy heat of the waterfront.

*

Poke Toholo braced himself against the side of the cab.

The truck driver, short, heavily built with freckles and a balding head yearned to talk to someone . . . anyone. Seeing Poke, standing on the highway, waving his thumb, he had pulled up and helped Poke get his rucksack into the cab. After Poke had settled, the truck roaring along the highway towards Paradise City, the driver began to talk.

'Man! You shouldn't be heading this way! You heard the radio? You didn't? Man! That's all I listen to, except when I'm home and have to listen to my wife! You heard about the Executioner? Yeah . . . something! Makes a change from the old crap I get on the radio . . . Nixon and trouble. Man! That really bends my ear, but this is different! Everyone for miles around is yakking about this killer. Where are you from? Jacksonville? Sure, I know it . . . not many towns on this highway I don't know. On vacation, huh? Well, you sure could be walking into trouble. This Executioner . . . I guess he's a nutter. Right now before I picked you up, the radio gave out the cops are looking for an Indian. Don't make any mistake about this . . . the cops are smart around here. They wouldn't give that out if they weren't sure it's an Indian who knocked off these slobs. Now look, I like Indians, but to me every Indian looks like any other Indian . . . you get what I mean? I'm no dope. I guess every white man looks like any white man to an Indian . . . makes sense, doesn't it? But imagine! An Indian knocking off these rich slobs! You want to know how I feel about it? I'll tell you: who the hell cares if three rich slobs get knocked off? It was on the radio like I said. This whore saw him: Mandy Lucas. She flops at the Pelota Club. Man! Could I tell you something about that joint! She saw this guy getting out of her car . . . that's something, isn't it? Her car! I stopped off at a café for a bite to eat and there she was on the telly ... on the telly! A whore! Okay, I wouldn't mind throwing her over. She has something! Those tits! So the cops are giving her protection. She says she can pick this guy any time and the cops are going to line up every goddamn Indian in the City so she can put the finger on one of them. How do you like that? I tell you, Man, this is a red hot City for an Indian ... so watch out!'

Poke, his face expressionless, but his black eyes on fire, said he would watch out.

*

Police Officer Wargate yawned, stretched his muscular arms and yearned for a cigarette. The time was 02.45. He had been in the parking lot behind the Pelota club now for the past two hours. He had had his instructions from Sergeant Beigler.

'Listen, Mike,' Beigler had said 'the only way up to the girl's room is by the fire escape. She's our only witness. Just make sure no one gets at her.'

Wargate's feet hurt. He didn't believe the girl was in any danger, but this was what he was paid for so he patrolled, yearned for a cigarette and pitied himself.

Poke came around the building like a black ghost, pressed against the wall in the deep shadows. He had a knife in his hand. He watched Wargate moving around and he waited.

The sound of drum beats and the strident notes of a saxophone came from the club.

Wargate stopped walking and leaned against the fire escape. He looked around the moonlit parking lot, crammed with cars. There would be no one around now until the club shut down – in another half an hour. He yielded to his need for a cigarette. As he struck a match, Poke threw the knife.

The wail of the saxophone drowned Wargate's cry. Poke moved forward, pulled out the knife, wiped it on Wargate's sleeve, then started up the fire escape.

Each of the six hostesses who had rooms on the top floor of the club had their names on their doors.

This was something their Agent had insisted on.

'Girls like to be thought stars,' he said while hammering out the contract with the manager of the club. 'You want them to be happy, don't you?'

So Poke had no trouble in finding Mandy Lucas's room.

The smell of stale perfume and sweat greeted him as he eased open the door.

Moonlight fell directly on the sleeping girl. Since she had become a star witness, Mandy no longer worked in the club. She spent her time sleeping which was a novelty to her.

She was dreaming of her TV triumph, living again that exciting moment when for the first time she had to face the television camera.

As Poke's gloved hand closed gently over her nose and mouth, she came awake. As her body arched in terror, his grip tightened brutally. He slid the razor sharp knife through her breast and into her heart.

Five

Walton Walbeck found amongst his mail the first of a number of notes that were to be received by other wealthy members of the Fifty Club during the week.

Walbeck tall, pale and effeminate, had inherited a considerable fortune from his father and apart from playing expert bridge, had never done a stroke of work in his life. Now at the age of sixty-five, he was a bore to his acquaintances – he had no friends – a bore also to himself and he was terrified of death.

He was more nervous than usual this morning as he ate a lightly boiled egg and read his mail. Mrs. Dunc Browler's horrible death had shocked him. He had heartily disliked the old woman, but as a bridge partner she had pleased him. To die like that! Horrible! Then this brash commentator talking on the eight o'clock news. *The police seem powerless to do anything.* That really worried him. Then this woman's murder ... Mandy something or other ... stabbed! And the police officer protecting her also stabbed! Protection! Was that what the police called protection!

His nerves jangled as he heard Jackson, his manservant, drop something in the kitchen.

74

He reached for another letter and found himself looking at an envelope, addressed to himself in smudgy printed letters that made him grimace in distaste. After hesitating, he slit open the envelope, extracted a sheet of notepaper and flicked the paper open.

Written in crude block letters was a message that set his heart thumping and icy fingers of fear up his spine.

Do You Want To Stay Alive?

Follow these instructions carefully:

Put five one hundred dollar bills in an envelope and fasten the envelope by tape to the bottom of the coin box in telephone booth A in the Airport lobby by 12.00 today.

Unless of course you'd rather be dead.

Police protection? Ask Mandy Lucas.

The Executioner.

Enclose this note with the money to insure your future safety.

Walbeck dropped the letter as if it had bitten him. In a surge of panic he jumped to his feet and started across the room to the telephone. Then he paused. His heart was now hammering so violently he felt faint.

'Jackson!' he cried and dropped into a chair. 'Jackson!'

His manservant who had endured him for ten years came unhurriedly to the door. He was a year or so younger than Walbeck but wore less well.

'Did you call, sir?'

Walbeck stared at him and realised with a sinking feeling that Jackson was not only useless but he might even be happy that this awful thing had happened to him. Walbeck had no illusions about Jackson's feelings towards him.

'No ... no ... go away! Don't stand staring at me! Get on with your work!'

'Yes, sir.'

When Jackson had gone, Walbeck forced himself to get to his feet. He went to the liquor cabinet and poured himself a stiff shot of brandy. He drank it, then waited until the liquor took hold. While he waited, his brain darted around in his head like a trapped mouse.

The Executioner!

He thought of McCuen and Mrs. Dunc Browler and the

woman Riddle had made his mistress ... now this Mandy woman!

The man was a lunatic and the police could do nothing!

Unsteadily, he crossed to the breakfast table and peered at the letter again.

Should he tell the police? Should he call his attorney? What could they do?

No ... the best thing ... the safest thing was to pay up. He would do it at once! He would go to the bank, get the money, then go to the airport. It wasn't as if this was a big sum of money ... five hundred dollars ... nothing!

*

Poke Toholo, carrying his rucksack, walked into the airport lobby and mingled with the crowd of waiting travellers. He found a vacant seat near the row of telephone booths and sat down, putting his rucksack between his feet. No one paid any attention to him: he immediately became part of the background. There were several Seminole Indians in flowered shirt and hipsters, in small groups, waiting for planes. Poke opened a newspaper and began to read the sports page.

A little after 11.30 he saw Walton Walbeck come into the lobby. He had seen him many times in the Fifty Club and immediately recognised him. He watched Walbeck head for telephone booth A. There was a girl using the telephone and Walbeck waited, looking around nervously, dabbing at his high temples with a silk handkerchief.

The girl finally finished her conversation and leaving the booth, she walked quickly away. Walbeck stepped into the booth and shut the glass door. His back concealed what he was doing. After a few moments, he came out, looked furtively from right to left, then hurried towards the exit.

Poke looked around the crowded lobby. He was tempted to go to the booth to see if the money was there, but he resisted the temptation. He was already taking a dangerous risk being here.

Had Walbeck told the police? Had they told him to carry out the instructions and were now waiting for someone to collect the money?

Again Poke looked around. He couldn't see anyone who looked like a cop, but that meant nothing. If Walbeck had told the police, the cops would keep out of sight but somewhere they would be watching the telephone booth, waiting to pounce.

He continued to read the newspaper. From time to time, people used booth A. The money – if it was there – would be strapped to the bottom of the coin box and who would be likely to find it if they weren't actually looking for it?

Finally, he got to his feet and walked casually to the exit where the buses waited to take passengers to the City.

He paused at the exit as if he had remembered something, then walked over to a telephone booth on the opposite side of the one used by Walbeck and shut himself in.

*

Chuck looked at his watch. The time was 11.45. He was sitting on the bed, smoking: a small pile of dead cigarette butts lay between his feet.

Meg sat on a chair by the window, watching the activity going on below. She knew Chuck was waiting for something but she now had learned not to ask questions.

The sound of the telephone bell made them both start.

Chuck snatched up the receiver.

'Chuck?'

He recognised Poke's voice.

'Yeah.'

'Airport . . . booth A,' Poke said and hung up.

Chuck replaced the receiver. A surge of excitement ran through him. He knew Poke wouldn't have telephoned unless he was sure the money was there . . . so it was working!

'You're going out,' Chuck said staring at Meg. 'Now listen carefully. Take the bus to the airport. You know where the bus station is?'

She nodded dumbly.

'When you get to the airport you go into the main lobby. On the right as you go in there's a row of telephone booths. Each booth is lettered: A.B.C. and so on. Go to booth A. Now listen carefully: dial this number.' He gave her a scrap of paper. 'That's the number of the Tourist Information centre in the City. You want to know where there's free bathing.'

Meg listened, her eyes growing wide.

'You've got to have a reason for using the booth,' Chuck went on. 'A cop might want to know. He might want to know why you're at the airport. Tell him you're on vacation and you thought it would be fun to take a look at the place ... tell him you like airports.' He studied her. 'No cop is going to ask you anything, but you have to have a story ready if you're unlucky. Do you get it?'

She nodded.

'Okay, now listen ... while you're dialling the number, feel under the coin box. Fastened to it by tape will be an envelope. Put the envelope in your bag. Don't let anyone see you do it. Understand?'

She licked her lips.

'Why don't you do it? Why me?' she asked huskily.

Chuck stared at her.

'Am I going to have trouble with you?'

She flinched.

'No ... I'll do it.'

'Fine. When you get the envelope you come right back here. Poke will be watching. Remember that.'

She looked at him, her expression wooden.

'Who's Poke?'

He grinned, then nodded.

'You're learning ... but remember you'll be watched. Now get going.'

She picked up her shabby handbag and left the room. He listened to the sound of her footfalls on the wooden stairs, then when he was sure she had gone, he ran down the stairs, nodded to the fat Indian sitting behind the desk and went out into the sunshine.

Moving swiftly through the crowd, he approached the bus station. When it was in sight, he paused behind a banana stall. He could see Meg with a small group of waiting people, then when the bus arrived, he watched her get in.

As soon as the bus left, he ran along the waterfront and to the parked Buick. Taking the side streets and driving fast, he arrived at the airport ten minutes ahead of the bus. He entered the airport lobby and looked around for a place where he could watch the row of telephone booths and yet be out of sight.

As he took up a position by a news stall, he saw Meg come hurrying in. He watched her as she walked to booth A and he nodded to himself.

No panic ... no sign of fear.

He watched her step into the booth and close the door. Then

the muscles in his stomach turned into a hard knot. Suddenly from nowhere two detectives appeared. Although in plain clothes, there was no mistaking them: big men, clean, smart, broad shouldered and purposeful. They cut through the crowd, moving towards the line of telephone booths and Chuck felt a trickle of sweat run down his face.

Would Meg give him away? That was his first thought. He'd better get the hell out of here and out of town! He was so scared he couldn't move, but just stood watching.

The detectives shifted away from the row of booths and pulled up in front of a young Seminole Indian who had just come into the lobby.

Chuck flicked sweat off his chin and drew in a long slow breath. He watched the Indian going with the detectives, protesting and waving his hands while people stared. The detectives herded the Indian into a corner and began shooting questions at him.

Chuck was in time to see Meg leave the telephone booth and walk towards the exit. She hadn't seen what had been going on, but she was walking a little too quickly to be casual.

Again Chuck felt a stab of fear.

If one of the cops saw her and wondered why she was almost running! But Chuck needn't have worried. The two detectives were too occupied in questioning the Indian.

Walking stiff legged, Chuck left the airport. He was in time to see Meg getting into a bus, then he hurried to where he had parked the Buick.

There were only five people in Meg's bus. She paid the fare, then walked to the far end of the bus where she was on her own. The bus driver had looked curiously at her. She knew she must look awful. Cold chills crawled up and down her spine, and as soon as she sat down, she began to shiver. She hoped none of the other passengers had noticed the state she was in. She sat for some minutes trying to control the shivering, then as the bus began to rattle onto the highway and she saw no one was turning to look at her, she began to relax a little.

She waited until the bus got caught up in the heavy traffic, then she opened her bag. She took from it the manila envelope she had found, taped under the coin box. She looked at it, turned it over, hesitated, then because she had to know, she took a nail file from her bag and with it, slit the envelope open.

She took from the envelope five one hundred dollar bills. The sight of all this money made her cringe with fear, then she found the note from the Executioner. Terror replaced fear. Saliva rushed into her mouth. For an awful moment she thought she was about to throw up, but somehow she managed to control the spasm. She read the note again, aware her body was oozing cold sweat.

So now she knew! So now what she had suspected had become a reality!

The Executioner!

Poke!

How many people had he killed? Her mind flinched as she tried to remember. But did it matter how many? One was enough!

With shaking hands she put the money and the note back into the envelope and the envelope back into the bag.

And Chuck was mixed up with this awful Indian . . . and she was too!

She stared through the dusty window, seeing the palm trees, the beaches and the bathers while her mind remained paralysed with terror.

Then she forced herself to think.

Poke was frightening people into paying him money and using her to collect the money! The police could have been waiting for her! They could have arrested her as she took the envelope from under the coin box!

Murder!

No! Chuck wasn't worth her getting mixed up with murder! Her mind darted here and there. What should she do? Again saliva rushed into her mouth: again she had to fight off throwing up.

Go to the police?

She shivered. The police! She imagined herself walking into the cop house and trying to tell them what was going on. Even if they believed her, what would they do? Send her back to her parents? More likely put her in some goddamn home in need of protection! Her mind banged around inside her skull like a pelota ball.

She crossed her legs and uncrossed them. She clenched her fists, beat them on her knees, then stopped, looking fearfully down the aisle of the bus. No one turned to stare at her. She wanted to scream at these five people: Help me!

There was only one thing to do, she told herself, forcing herself into calmness. She must go to Miami right away. From Miami she must travel north as far from Paradise City as she could get. She must get lost: forget Chuck, start all over again.

Once she had come to this decision, she began to think without panic.

Okay, she thought, I've got that fixed. A couple of miles ahead of her was a Greyhound bus station. She would ask the driver to drop her off. She would take the Greyhound to Miami. From there . . .

Cold fingers of despair gripped her.

All her clothes were in that awful room run by that fat Indian! She had nothing. What was she thinking about? How could she get to Miami? She had less than two dollars in her bag!

For some moments she sat staring out of the window.

Two dollars? What was the matter with her? She had five hundred dollars! Dare she use this money? Wouldn't it make her an accessory or whatever the cops called it? But to get away! To escape from this nightmare! She would be crazy not to use the money!

She drew in a long shuddering breath.

With five hundred dollars she could get to New York. She'd be safe there . . . and she could get work!

Her shivering ceased and her confidence in herself returned. Furtively, she opened her bag and fingered the five one hundred dollar bills without taking them from the envelope.

She would do it!

Her body jerked with a suppressed sob of relief.

No more Chuck! No more Poke! No more police!

Determined not to have second thoughts, she closed the bag, got up and walked down the aisle to the driver.

'Would you please stop at the Greyhound station?' she said, surprised how steady her voice was. 'It's not far, is it?'

The bus driver was a father of five daughters. They were all nice, good, clean kids: the eldest about this girl's age, he thought. Well, he was lucky! Thank God, his girls were decent. This girl! He could smell Meg's stale sweat. He looked at the dirty clothes she had on. Thank God, he wasn't her father!

'Yeah . . . about two minutes,' he said looking away from her. 'I'll stop.'

'Thank you,' Meg said and went back to her seat.

81

A few minutes later the bus slid to a stop outside the busy Greyhound bus station.

Meg was already coming down the aisle as the bus slowed. She forced a smile as she climbed down the three steep steps of the bus.

'Thank you.'

'And thank *you*,' the driver said with heavy sarcasm. He engaged gear and the bus moved on.

Clutching her handbag, Meg started towards the ticket office.

'Hi!'

The sound hit her like a knife thrusts into her heart. She turned, her body suddenly icy cold.

Chuck was leaning out of the window of the Buick. He was grinning.

'Do you want a ride, baby?' he asked.

*

Elliot Hansen was considered one of the great bridge players of the world, but the fact he was a blatant homosexual and cared nothing about competition bridge, he was content to be secretary of the Fifty Club.

On this hot, sunny afternoon, he was behind his desk, regarding Detective Lepski the way you regard a large, hairy spider that has dropped unexpectedly into your bath.

Elliot Hansen was tall, handsome and impressive to look at. His thick white hair fell to his collar. His perfect dentures, cleaned at least three times a day, gleamed when he smiled. He claimed to be sixty years of age, but if you added seven years you could still be off target. He dealt only with the very rich. He lived in luxury and would drink only '29 or '59 chateau bottled wine. He lived in the small world of luxury in the Club, but was not adverse, even now, to a quick fumble in a toilet with any pretty youth who caught his eye.

Chief of Police Terrell had decided if anyone could handle Hansen it would be Lepski who was down to earth, no snob, unimpressed by riches and above all, ambitious.

'Yes?' Hansen asked in his soft, melodious voice. He took a scented silk handkerchief from his cuff and waved it before his elegant nose.

In his cop voice that made Hansen wince, Lepski explained why he was here.

Elliot Hansen was English. Many years ago he had been the major domo to a Duke, until the Duke got into trouble with a boy scout. Then when the English police had become tiresome about Hansen's own activities, he had left the country and had been pleased to accept the position of Secretary to the most exclusive bridge club in Florida.

Hansen listened to what Lepski was saying, scarcely believing he could be hearing aright.

'But, my good fellow, that's most unlikely! One of our servants? No! No! Unthinkable!'

Lepski hated homosexuals as much as Hansen hated detectives. He moved impatiently.

'We're looking for an Indian,' he said. 'The description we have is he's around twenty-three to -five years of age, thick black hair, and wears a flowered shirt and dark hipsters. Have you an Indian working here who matches this description?'

'So young?' Hansen winced. 'No ... no ... all our Indian servants are elderly. They have worked here for years ... really years, and as for wearing a flowered shirt.' He threw back his head and laughed. To Lepski the sound he made was like the neighing of a mare.

'Yeah ... but look at it from our angle,' Lepski said. 'Two of your club members have been killed. A third one has knocked himself off: his girl friend killed. We're wondering if there's a connection between this killer and this club. We know he is a Seminole Indian. You follow me? Maybe one of your staff is gunning for your members.'

Hansen revealed his dentures in a supercilious smile.

'I assure you, my dear fellow ... quite, quite wrong thinking. Our servants have been with us for years ... but, years. They love us all. You can have no idea. These Indians are very loyal. They really love us.'

'Couldn't one of them possibly have a grudge against the club?' Lepski persisted. 'Someone who imagines he's had a bad deal?'

'A bad deal?' Hansen was genuinely shocked. 'The staff here are always treated splendidly. We're just a big, happy family.'

Lepski breathed heavily through his nose.

'Did you ever have reason to dismiss one of your staff? Someone, maybe, who didn't come up to your standard?'

Hansen was toying with his gold fountain pen. It slipped out of his fingers and rolled across his desk. He gave a little start as if he had a twinge of toothache. This reaction wasn't lost on Lepski.

There was a long pause, then Hansen picked up his pen and began to toy with it again.

'Well, I suppose ... in the past ... yes, that's possible,' he said slowly and reluctantly.

His mind went back to the young Indian. How long ago was it ... four months? Until this moment he had put the incident out of his mind, now the memory came back with frightening clarity. What was his name? Toholo? Yes ... his father had been working in the Club for twenty years. He remembered the old man coming to him and asking if his son could work at the Club. When he had seen him, he had agreed ... a lovely, beautifully built boy! But what a savage! That moment when he had smiled at him ... they had been alone in the washroom and when he had touched him. Hansen flinched. What a savage! It had been frightening. Of course he had been carried away. The boy had looked so deceptive. He had had to get rid of him. He had been careful to explain to his father that the boy was out of place in the Club ... too young. The old man had stared at him. Hansen shifted uneasily in his chair. He could still see the contempt in the black eyes.

But he couldn't possibly tell this ghastly detective about Toholo. The moment he attempted to explain ... no! It was impossible!

'Do you remember any particular Indian you had to get rid of?' Lepski repeated.

The hard cop voice jarred on Hansen's nerves.

'It hasn't happened in years,' he said. 'You know how it is.' He looked at Lepski, then his eyes shifted. 'Of course they get old. Then we pension them off.'

Lepski knew he was onto something.

'Do you keep a register of your staff?'

Hansen blinked. He took out his silk handkerchief and touched his temples.

'Of course.'

'Can I see it?'

'But I assure you, you're wasting your time.'

Lepski leaned back in his chair. His lean face made Hansen think of a hawk.

'I got paid to waste time,' he said. 'Or don't you want me to see it?'

Hansen felt suddenly faint. He drew on his dignity.

'I must ask you not to be impertinent,' he said, his voice unsteady. 'If you want to see the register, you may.'

Lepski's cop eyes stared bleakly.

'That's what I want to see.'

'Well, of course.'

Hansen opened a drawer in his desk. He passed a leather bound book across to Lepski.

Lepski studied the list of names which meant nothing to him, but he was now convinced Hansen was attempting to conceal something.

'I'd like a copy of this. We'll want to talk to all these men,' he said curtly and dropped the book on the desk.

'Of course.'

Hansen sat motionless. The two men looked at each other, then Lepski said, 'I'll wait.'

'Of course.'

Hansen got shakily to his feet, took the book and went through a door into the outer office. Some five minutes later, he returned and handed a sheet of paper to Lepski.

'There you are . . . it won't help, but there you are.'

Lepski studied the list of names, then he looked up and stared bleakly at Hansen.

'There's one missing,' he said. 'From your register, you have fifteen Indians working for you. There are only fourteen names here.'

Hansen's face sagged.

'Excuse me . . . you have no idea the trouble I have with my staff. My secretary is almost an idiot.'

'Is that right?' Lepski held out his hand for the register which Hansen was still holding. His face now pale, Hansen gave it to him.

Lepski checked the names from the register against the list Hansen had given him.

'Toholo? Who is he?' he asked.

Hansen licked his dry lips.

'Did she leave Toholo's name off the list? How extraordinary! He's our oldest and most trusted! I assure you you don't have to give him a thought. Toholo! Why he must have been with us for twenty years!'

Lepski got to his feet.

'Okay ... sorry to have troubled you.' He started to the door, then paused, 'Would it worry you if I talked to Toholo right now?'

Hansen sank into his chair. He picked up his gold pen and stared at it. He now looked older than his years and that made him look very old.

'So long as you don't inconvenience the members of this club, you may talk to him,' he said huskily. 'You will find him in the bar.'

'And where's that?'

Hansen continued to stare at the gold pen.

'At the far end of the corridor: the door on your left.'

Then he braced himself. He must make an effort, he told himself. He just couldn't let the life he had made for himself be shattered. He looked up and stared desperately at Lepski. 'But I do assure you ... you will be wasting your time.'

'Yeah ... you said that before,' Lepski said and left the room.

Hansen dropped the pen. Sick fear gripped him. His mind went back twenty years when he had had a telephone call from a good friend warning him the police were making inquiries about him and he had better get out of England ... the same sick feeling he had hoped he would never experience again.

But he was to experience it yet again the following morning when he received a letter asking him if he wanted to stay alive. The letter, demanding five hundred dollars was signed: The Executioner.

*

Chuck drove the Buick down a dirt road that led to one of the many beaches along the coast. It was one of the less popular beaches because of the sand dunes, but already there were other cars there and people in the sea.

Chuck parked the car away from the rest of the cars. He turned to look at Meg who sat huddled away from him. They hadn't spoken during the short drive to the beach.

'Did you get it?' he asked.

With shaking hands, she opened her bag, took out the envelope and gave it to him.

'So you looked?' he said when he saw the envelope was open. He took out the five one hundred dollar bills. 'Nice,' he said under his breath. 'Beautiful bread!'

Meg shivered.

The letter from the Executioner fluttered out from between the bills and landed on the bench seat.

'You saw this too?'

Meg put her clenched fists between her knees. Words wouldn't come. She just stared at Chuck.

'Where were you going, baby?' Chuck asked. 'Miami?'

She nodded, then making the effort, she said, 'I won't have anything more to do with this!' Her voice was a husky croak. 'I'm quitting! I won't say a thing! I promise! But I'm quitting!'

'Oh, sure.' Chuck folded the bills and put them in his shirt pocket. 'Lots of freaks quit . . . some are lucky . . . but you won't be, baby.'

She beat her fists together as she stared frantically at him.

'I promise! I won't say a thing! Just let me go! This Indian is sick in the head! Do you want to get mixed up with a crazy Indian?' Again she put her fists between her knees as she rocked to and fro. 'Chuck! Think! Let's get away! He's murdering people! Please, Chuck, listen to me!'

A large red and white beach ball dropped out of the sky, bounced on the wing of the car and then hit the windshield.

Both Chuck and Meg flinched back.

A small boy, wearing a tiny slip, his thin body browned by the sun, came running up to capture the ball. He grinned at Chuck as he picked up the ball.

'Sorry, mister,' the kid said, paused, then went on. 'You want to have a kick?'

'Sure.' Chuck got out of the car. Taking the ball from the kid, he bounced it on the sand, then kicked it high into the air. With a squeal of delight, the kid went chasing after the ball as it floated towards the sea.

Chuck got back into the car.

'Nice kid,' he said. 'You know something? When I was his age I never had a ball . . . I never had a goddamn thing.'

'I want to quit!' Meg said, her voice shrill. 'Will you listen! I'm quitting!'

Chuck picked up the Executioner's note and read it, then he looked at her.

'Do you want to stay alive, baby?' he asked.

She seemed to shrink inside her clothes and she huddled further away from him.

'Do I have to spell it out?' he went on. 'Okay, so he's crazy. It's your bad luck. It could be my bad luck too. You take off if that's the way you feel about it, but you won't get far. When you are stuck with a crazy Indian, you're stuck with something special. But if you want to take off, go ahead, but ask yourself how far you'll get. Okay, so suppose you get as far as Miami? I don't see how you'll do that without money, but suppose you do? What's the good of getting to Miami if you land up with a knife in your guts or a slug in your head?' He tapped the letter. 'You read this, didn't you? Ask yourself the same question: do you want to stay alive?'

Meg lifted her hair off her shoulders in a frantic gesture of indecision.

'You can't frighten me! I don't care! I'm quitting!'

Chuck began to pick his nose.

'You know something? You're beginning to bore me. Go ahead . . . quit. Get the hell out of this car, but there's one thing I won't do . . .'

She stared at him.

'I won't buy one goddamn flower for your funeral,' he concluded.

'Hi, mister!'

The kid was back again.

Chuck grinned at him.

'You want another kick, mister?'

Chuck looked at Meg.

'Piss off . . . I've got company.'

He got out of the car and taking the ball he kicked it high into the air. Then he ran with the kid towards the sea and as the ball bounced, he let the kid have it, then snatched the ball away and again kicked it towards the sea.

Meg watched them.

Loneliness, the hopelessness of facing a future without anything and fear kept her in the car.

She was still there when Chuck had finished the ball game with the kid and came strolling back to her.

*

The half mile of stalls along the waterfront made up the City's market: everything of local produce was sold there from bananas, oranges to turtles, shrimps and even sponges. Each stall had its gay-multi-coloured awning. Most of the stall holders were Indians.

Poke Toholo stood behind a stall loaded with oranges. The stall was owned by an Indian named Jupiter Lucie.

Lucie was a small happy rubber ball of a man who hated rich people and hated the police, but he had been smart enough to steer clear of trouble. He was known as a 'safe' man on the waterfront as he never asked questions nor busied himself with any affairs except his own. When Poke came to him and said he wanted a job without pay, Lucie had made an instant decision. He knew Poke's father. He knew Poke was a rebel. He knew Poke would never ask him for a job without pay unless he wanted a cover. He agreed, without hesitation.

So when two sweating plain clothes detectives finally came around to the stall, Lucie was there to explain away Poke's presence.

The detectives knew their assignment was hopeless anyway. They had trudged down the hot half mile, pausing at the stalls, asking questions and taking names but they knew a check up on the Indians was just so much waste of time.

'He's my cousin,' Lucie said, showing his gold capped teeth in a happy smile when the detectives asked about Poke. 'He's a very good boy ... like me. We have the same name ... Lucie. He's Joe and I'm Jupiter.'

The detectives wrote the names down and moved on, knowing it was so much water under the bridge.

Lucie and Poke exchanged smiles.

But Detective Max Jacoby who had been detailed to check all out-lying motels was a little more successful.

Mrs. Bertha Harris disliked all policemen. Some thirty years ago, she had been caught stealing goods from a Self-service store and she was never to forget the treatment she had received from the cop who took her in. So when Jacoby arrived at the Welcome motel, she decided to be as bloody minded as she could.

As usual she was munching a hamburger. She liked hamburgers the way old Sam made them with more onions than meat, but they were messy things to eat: she had to admit that.

'We're looking for an Indian,' Jacoby said without much hope. 'Age around twenty-five: thick black hair, tall and wearing a flowered shirt and dark hipsters.' He had said the same thing thirty times during the day and had got nowhere, but he was a trier ... this, he kept telling himself, was police work. 'Have you had a man like that staying with you?'

Bertha belched behind her hand.

'What was that again?'

Jacoby repeated what he had said.

Bertha thought while she breathed onion fumes in Jacoby's face.

'I get people,' she said finally. 'They come and go. If I could remember everyone who stays here I could make a fortune as an act on the telly, couldn't I?'

'Does that mean you have a lot of Indians staying here?' Jacoby asked, recognising that this fat old bitch was going to be difficult.

Bertha bit into the hamburger, chewed and stared vacantly past Jacoby.

'No ... can't say I do.'

'This is important,' Jacoby said, his voice hardening. 'We're investigating a murder case. I'm asking you if you have had a young Indian staying with you.'

Bertha chased a slab of meat from a back tooth with the aid of her little finger.

'I don't know anything about murder: that's for the cops to handle.'

'I'm asking you: have you had a young Indian staying with you recently?'

Murder!

Bertha suddenly lost her cool. As much a she wanted to remain unco-operative she realised this was serious.

'Sure ... I did have an Indian staying here.'

It took Jacoby ten minutes to drag from her a description but when he got it, it so fitted the man they were looking for, he had to restrain his excitement.

'Did he sign in?'

'Everyone has to sign in,' Bertha said virtuously and handed over a tattered book.

'Harry Lukon? This his name?'

'Yeah.'

'And these other two: Mr. and Mrs. Jack Allen?'

'Nice young people. They came with him in the car.'

'Cabins 4 and 5 ... right?'

Bertha sighed.

'Yeah.'

'I'll use your phone,' Jacoby said.

'Just make yourself at home,' Bertha said bitterly.

Jacoby talked to Beigler back at headquarters. Beigler listened, then said he would send the Homicide squad down to the motel right away.

'Stick around, Max . . . this sounds good.'

Jacoby hung up.

'Don't tell me,' Bertha said in disgust. 'Now I'm going to have cops around here like flies.'

Jacoby smiled at her.

'That is an understatement, Mrs. Harris,' he said.

*

At this time in the afternoon, the luxurious bar at the Fifty Club was deserted.

Lepski found Boca Toholo on his own. He was quietly arranging dishes of olives, salted almonds and the like in cut glass dishes for the rush hour which would begin in a couple of hours.

Boca Toholo was a small, thin man with greying hair, his eyes like jet beads. When he saw Lepski come into the dimly lit room, he put down a can of salted almonds and his wrinkled dark face became expressionless. He knew a police officer when he saw one. The very idea that a police officer should be here in this holy of holies warned him that this was something serious. But he had a clear conscience and he faced Lepski without flinching.

'You Toholo?' Lepski asked.

'Yes, sir . . . that is my name,' the old man said quietly.

'I'm Lepski . . . police headquarters.' Lepski climbed on a stool. He rested his elbows on the polished bar and regarded the Indian with a searching, but not hostile stare.

'Yes, sir.'

'I've been talking to Mr. Hansen,' Lepski said. 'His memory doesn't seem so good. I thought maybe you might help me.'

The old man filled another dish with almonds.

After a pause, Lepski went on, 'I asked Mr. Hansen if a young Indian, around twenty-three with thick black hair ever worked here. Mr. Hansen couldn't remember. Can you tell me?'

Toholo looked up.

'Would you be speaking of my son, sir?'

Lepski hadn't imagined it would be this easy.

'Your son? Does he work here?'

The old man shook his head.

'He had a promising career here. He is an excellent barman: better than I am. He has talent, but Mr. Hansen thought he was too young so he was sent away.'

Lepski looked searchingly at the old man. The stoney look of hatred in the Indian's eyes wasn't lost on him.

'Where is your son now, Toholo?'

'That I don't know, sir. He left the City. I haven't heard from him for four or five months. I am hoping he has a good job in some bar. He has talent.'

'How long did he work here before Mr. Hansen decided he was too young?'

'How long? About nine weeks.'

'Did anyone else beside Mr. Hansen think he was too young for the job?'

'No, sir. No one complained about my son.'

Lepski chewed his thumb nail while he thought.

'Was there some kind of trouble between Mr. Hansen and your son?' he asked finally.

'That is not my business, sir.'

That shut that door, Lepski thought.

'Tell me about your son, Toholo. Why hasn't he written to you? Didn't you and he get along?'

Toholo stared down at his dark, thin hands.

'Is my son in trouble, sir?'

Lepski hesitated. Then he decided he had everything to gain by putting his cards face up. He would risk the doors being slammed in his face, but he could be lucky.

'You've read about the Executioner?'

The old man looked up and stared at Lepski.

'Yes, sir.'

'We know this killer is an Indian,' Lepski said gently. 'He has killed two members of this club and a woman connected with another member of the club. This man is sick in the head. We've got to find him before he kills someone else. We know he is young. We're hunting for a lead. So I'm asking you what kind of boy your son is?'

The old man's face turned a mottled grey.

'You think my son could have done such things, sir?'

'I'm not saying that. We have to check. We're trying to find a sick Indian who seems to have inside information about the members of this club. Just what was the trouble between Hansen and your son?'

With a look of despair on his face, Toholo picked up a glass and began to polish it. Lepski saw his hands were unsteady.

'I know nothing about trouble, sir. Mr. Hansen thought my son was too young for a position here.'

'Have you a photograph of your son?'

The old man stiffened. He put down the glass, then forced himself to pick up another.

'No, sir. We Indians seldom have our photographs taken.'

'How did your son get along with the members of this Club?'

Watching the old man, Lepski felt instinctively that his questions were breaking him down. If he kept at it, he told himself, something would come out.

'What was that, sir?' Toholo asked huskily.

Lepski repeated his question.

Toholo seemed to shrink a little.

'I had hopes, sir, that my son would accept the conditions one must accept to be a good servant here, but, at times, he found it difficult.'

Lepski turned this over in his mind.

'What you're saying is your son found these rich old jerks hard to take?'

Toholo looked shocked.

'No, sir ... nothing like that. My son is young. Young people...' He stopped, making a helpless gesture.

Lepski was feeling sorry for this old man. He saw he was trying so hard to be loyal to his son.

'Has he ever been in trouble with the police?'

The jet black eyes widened.

'Thank God, no, sir.'

Lepski paused, then asked, 'Has he been in any kind of trouble?'

Toholo put down the glass he was polishing. He stared down at the glass and the sadness on his face made Lepski uneasy. After a long pause, Lepski repeated his question.

'My son has a difficult temper, sir,' the old man said huskily. 'He has been difficult at home. I had to speak to our doctor. He did speak to Poke, but ... young people are difficult these days.'

'Who is your doctor?'

'My doctor?' Toholo looked up. 'Why, Dr. Wanniki.'

Lepski took out his notebook and wrote the name down, then he leaned forward and looked directly at Toholo.

'Is your son sick, Mr. Toholo?'

The old man suddenly sank onto a stool and put his hands to his face.

'Yes, God help his mother and me . . . yes, he could be.'

Six

While the Homicide squad were systematically turning over the two cabins at the Welcome motel, Lepski drove back to headquarters.

With the siren screaming, Lepski stormed down the busy boulevard, imagining himself to be Jim Clark coming into the last lap. If there was one thing Lepski loved more than anything else it was to cut a swathe through the Rolls, and Bentleys and the Cadillacs of the rich. He watched the sleek, glittering cars pull to one side in panic as his siren hit their drivers. He flashed by the wealthy with their fat plum-coloured faces and their immaculate clothes and grinned his wolf's grin. This was, he thought, as he whipped his car by a semi-paralysed owner of a Silver Shadow Rolls, a compensation for the dreary, hard toil he had saddled himself with as a police officer.

He had to restrain himself from leaning out of his car window and yelling, 'Up yours!' as he swept down the boulevard.

He arrived outside headquarters, swept through the gateway and into the police yard. He shut off the siren, wiped his face with the back of his hand and scrambled out of the car. He ran across the yard and started up the stairs, then suddenly he realised how tired he was.

He paused for a moment to think. It occurred to him he hadn't been home for two nights and for fifty-eight hours, he hadn't thought of his wife. He also realised he had had only four hours' sleep since he had left her and those four hours had been spent on a truckle bed at headquarters.

He shook his head, then started up the steps again. He arrived in the Charge room where Sergeant Charlie Tanner was coping with the everyday events of a busy cop house.

'Charlie! Did you think to call my wife?' Lepski demanded, coming to a skidding stop before Tanner's desk.

'How could I forget?' Tanner said with some bitterness. 'I didn't have to call her. She has been calling *me*! You'll have to speak to her, Tom. She's blocking our lines.'

'Yeah.' Lepski ran his fingers through his hair. 'Did she sound worked up?'

Tanner considered this while he sucked the end of his biro.

'I wouldn't know what you call worked up,' he said finally, 'but to me, she sounded like a tiger with a bee up its arse.'

Lepski closed his eyes, then opened them.

'Look, Charlie, be a pal. Call her: tell her I'm working non-stop. Will you do that for me?'

'Not me!' Tanner said firmly. 'I want to keep my ear drums intact.'

Lepski released a snort down his nostrils that would have startled El Cordes.

'Who cares about your goddamn ear drums? Call her! Didn't I call your wife when you had your back to the wall? Didn't I?'

Tanner wilted. He remembered the awful occasion when he had had it off with a strawberry blonde and Lepski, by bare faced lying, had saved his marriage.

'That's blackmail, Tom!'

'So go ahead and file charges,' Lepski snarled. 'Call Carroll and pour the oil,' then he started up the stairs to the Detectives' room.

Within minutes he was reporting to Captain Terrell with Beigler sitting in.

'Okay, Tom, you go talk to this doctor ... what's his name. Wanniki? If this boy is as sick as his father thinks he is then he must be our number one.' Terrell turned to Beigler. 'Get someone down to Toholo's home. We might find a photograph of this boy and we could find his finger prints.' He got to his feet. 'I'll go down to the Fifty Club and talk to some of the members.'

As Lepski started down the stairs, passing the Charge room,

95

he saw Tanner waving frantically as he held out the telephone receiver.

Lepski pulled up short, skidding on his heels.

'What is it?'

'Your wife,' Tanner said.

One look at Tanner's stricken face gave Lepski cramps in his stomach. He hesitated, then snatched the receiver from Tanner's hand.

'Carroll? I have been meaning to call, honey. Right now I'm up to my ears and over the top of my head! I'll call you some time. Okay?... okay? I've got to go out right this second!'

'Lepski!'

The tone of his wife's voice was like a bullet through Lepski's brain.

He winced, then resigned himself.

'Yeah ... yeah ... how are you, baby? I'm rushing around like a goddamn ... I mean, I'm busy, baby!'

'Lepski! Will you stop yammering and listen to me?'

Lepski leaned on Tanner's desk and dragged his tie loose.

'I told you ... I'm sorry ... I have had only four hours' sleep since I saw you. I ... Goddamn it! I'm busy!'

'If I didn't think for one moment that you were, are and will be busy, Lepski, I would divorce you,' Carroll said. 'Now will you stop sounding off and let me sound off?'

Lepski tried to make holes in the surface of Tanner's desk with his fingers and nearly succeeded.

'I'm listening,' he said.

'I've just seen Mehitabel Bessinger.'

'Have you given away another bottle of my whisky?'

'Will you stop thinking about your drink. Mehitabel knew this Indian was the Executioner! She told me and I told you, but you wouldn't listen! She...'

'Just a moment ... did you give her a bottle of my goddamn whisky?'

'Lepski! How many more times do I have to ask you not to use vulgar language?'

The expression on Lepski's face so startled Sergeant Tanner that he instinctively reached for the emergency Red Cross box.

'Yeah. So what did the old rum-dum foretell?'

'Don't call her names like that. If I were you, I'd be ashamed to call an old woman a name like that.'

Lepski made a noise like a car with a flat battery trying to start.

'What was that?' Even Carroll who was used to the noises her husband made was startled. 'Are you all right, Lepski?'

'I don't know.'

'There are times when I get worried about you. You don't seem to be able to concentrate and to become a sergeant you have to concentrate.'

Lepski wiped the sweat off his face.

'Yeah . . . you're right. Go ahead . . . I'm concentrating.'

'Thank goodness! Mehitabel says . . . you're sure you're listening?'

Lepski stamped on his own foot with exasperation and hurt himself. As he began to hop up and down, Tanner who had never taken his eyes off Lepski, sat back stunned, his eyes goggling.

'Yes, I'm listening,' Lepski said, holding his foot in the air.

'She says you must look for the Executioner among oranges.'

'Among who?' Lepski shouted.

'Don't shout like that: it's vulgar. I said she said you should look for this man among oranges. She sees that in her crystal ball.'

'She does? Among oranges, huh?' Lepski drew in a breath that would have made a Hoover cleaner green with envy. 'Well, that's something. She can't go wrong with a give-out like that, can she? Let's face it: the whole of this goddamn district is stinking with oranges. She's on a winner there, isn't she? For that, did she grab another bottle of my whisky?'

'I'm telling you what she said. She was right the first time, but you didn't believe her. This is her second clue. Use your head, Lepski.'

'Okay, baby, I'll use it. I've got to go now.'

'I'm trying to help you get promoted.'

'Sure . . . yeah . . . yeah . . . thanks!' He paused, then went on, 'You didn't answer my question. Did that old fruit vendor get another bottle of my whisky?'

There was a long pause, then Carroll said, her voice icy, 'There are times, Lepski, when I think you have a tiny mind,' and she hung up.

Lepski replaced the receiver and stared at Tanner.

'Did your wife ever tell you you had a tiny mind, Charlie?'

Tanner gaped at him.

'Why should she? She wouldn't know what the word means.'

'Yeah. You're lucky,' and Lepski went down the stairs three at the time and threw himself into his car.

*

The hot evening sun beat down on the quay, bouncing off the striped awnings of the fruit stalls. The serious buying was over. A few stragglers, hoping to get cheap fruit, still moved around the stalls, but the main business of the day was over.

Jupiter Lucie had gone across to a nearby bar for a beer, leaving Poke in charge of the stall. They had had a good day and the stall had only a few boxes of oranges left.

Chuck came out of the shadows and paused by the stall. The two men looked at each other. The glittering black eyes of the Indian and Chuck's small, uneasy eyes surveyed the quay, then Chuck moved forward.

'I got it: five hundred bucks!'

'Is she all right?'

Chuck nodded.

Poke began to weigh a pound of oranges, taking his time.

'She'll be busy tomorrow,' he said as he took an orange off the scales and looked for a smaller one. 'Five calls.'

Chuck sucked in his breath.

'Five calls . . . *five*?'

'Two thousand five hundred dollars. I've put the dope how she's to collect it at the bottom of the sack.'

Chuck nodded. Then he looked along the quay to right and left, then when he was satisfied no one was watching him, he slid something into Poke's hand.

'I got it right: three fifty for you and a hundred and fifty for me?'

'Yes.'

Chuck picked up the sack of oranges and walked away.

After a while Lucie came from the bar. He and Poke began to dismantle the stall.

Tomorrow would be another day.

*

When Captain Terrell drove into the forecourt of the Fifty Club he was lucky to spot Rodney Branzenstein getting out of his Rolls.

98

Branzenstein was one of the founder members of the Club. Apart from being a top class bridge player he was also a top class Corporation lawyer.

The two men shook hands.

'What are you doing here, Frank? Don't tell me you're joining this mausoleum?'

'I'm looking for information,' Terrell said.

'Couldn't have come to a better man.' Branzenstein smiled. 'Come in and have a drink.'

'I'd rather sit in your swank car and talk,' Terrell said. 'It's my bet this mausoleum as you call it could be a little sensitive to a police visit.'

'You could be right.' Branzenstein led the way to his car, opened the door and slid in.

'Nice car: television ... phone ... air conditioning ... booze ... some car,' Terrell said, as he settled himself beside Branzenstein.

'You know how it is ... a status symbol. Between you and me, I'd rather drive an Avis,' Branzenstein said. 'It's part of the racket. What's on your mind, Frank?'

Terrell told him.

'Poke Toholo? Yes, I remember him: good looking and mixed one of the best martinis in this City. The trouble, of course, was old mother Hansen couldn't keep his hands to himself and the boy had to go.'

'I guessed that,' Terrell said. 'How did the other members of the club react to him ... apart from Hansen?'

Branzenstein shrugged.

'Ninety per cent of them don't believe anyone who isn't white isn't a monkey. Personally, I like Seminole Indians. But the majority of the members of the club regard Indians as fetch-and-carry monkeys.'

'Did Toholo ever have trouble with Mrs. Dunc Browler?'

'Come to think of it, he did,' Branzenstein said, his eyes narrowing. 'Of course she was a sad old bitch. All she thought about was her dog and bridge. I remember I was playing at another table ... this must be three months ago ... could be more ... I forget. Anyway, Toholo was serving drinks and Mrs. B. told him to take her dog out to have a pee. Toholo said he couldn't leave the bar. I heard it all. Maybe he didn't act servile as Mrs. B. expected. Anyway, she called him a nigger.'

'Then what happened?'

'The other three players with her told Toholo to take the dog out and not be insolent . . . so he took the dog out.'

'Who were the other players?'

'Riddle, McCuen and Jefferson Lacey.'

Terrell brooded.

'This makes a pattern, doesn't it?' he said finally. 'McCuen, Riddle and his mistress and Mrs. Browler are dead. I'd like to talk to Jefferson Lacey.'

Branzenstein nodded.

'Okay. He is one of our special members. He has a room at the club. Do you want me to introduce you?'

'That would be a help.'

But when Branzenstein asked the Hall porter if Mr. Lacey was available, he was told Mr. Lacey had gone out some thirty minutes ago.

Neither Branzenstein nor Terrell could guess that at this moment Jefferson Lacey, his face panic stricken, was fixing an envelope containing five one hundred dollar bills to the bottom of a coin box in a telephone booth in the lobby of the City's railroad station.

*

Meg was beyond caring as she walked into the busy lobby of the Excelsior hotel that catered for second class tourists.

The previous evening Chuck had told her she was to collect five envelopes from five different telephone booths the following morning.

'This is where we move into the money, baby,' Chuck had said. 'This is when you make the big discovery. Do you know what that is?'

Meg sat on the bed, staring down at the worn carpet. She said nothing.

'Baby . . . have you wax in your ears?'

The threat in his voice forced her to look up.

'What discovery?' she asked indifferently.

Chuck nodded his approval.

'You make the discovery like this Columbus or whatever his name was . . . you've reached the promised land . . . a meal ticket.'

She looked beyond Chuck and through the open window at the sky with its pink clouds that were slowly turning to crimson as the sun began to set.

100

'Is that what you are?' she asked.

'Yeah. That's what I am.' Chuck grinned. 'Every doll in this goddamn world is looking for a meal ticket and you've hit the jackpot. You've found a meal ticket . . . me!'

Meg continued to stare at the clouds as they turned blood red in the dying rays of the sun.

'Is that what you call it? I take all the risks, give you the money and you call yourself a meal ticket?' she said.

Chuck lit another cigarette.

'The trouble with you is you have nothing between your ears except an empty hole. You're lucky I have brains. Tomorrow, you go to five telephone booths and you pick up five hundred dollars from each booth. What does that add up to? Go on . . . tell me?'

'Who cares?' Meg said, shrugging. 'Why bother me?'

Chuck's hand flashed out.

Meg found herself lying flat on her back across the bed, her face stinging from the slap he had given her.

'You tell me,' he said viciously. 'Make with the addition!'

She touched the side of her face as she stared up at him. The imprints of his fingers showed on her white cheek.

'I don't know and I don't care,' she said and closed her eyes.

His second slap jolted her head.

'How much, baby?'

She lay there, waiting and shivering, her eyes tightly closed.

'Okay, okay, if you're that dumb!' Chuck said in disgust. 'You know something? You bore me. You've got no ambition. Tomorrow, you're picking up two thousand five hundred dollars? Do you hear? Two thousand five hundred dollars! Then you and me are getting the hell out of here! With that kind of money we're fixed!'

She suddenly realised what he was saying and what it meant and she felt a tiny surge of hope.

'What about him?' she asked, opening her eyes.

'So you've got something between your ears after all.' Chuck wagged his head in mock admiration. 'You know something? That's the first bright thing you've said since I found you.'

Found me?

Meg stared up at the dirty ceiling. Found me . . . like a lost dog or a stray cat. Yes . . . that's what she was . . . lost.

'Will you quit acting like a zombie and listen to me?' Chuck was saying.

It was good to lie flat on the bed, feeling the evening breeze coming through the open window on her hot, aching face. It required no effort. Even having to listen to Chuck's harsh voice required no effort.

'This Indian is crazy in the head ... he's a nutter,' Chuck went on. 'I never told you, but he could have killed me. The first time ... remember? When we went swimming.'

Why did he bother to tell her this now? she wondered. It was stale news. She had already told him the Indian was sick.

'So he's a nutter,' Chuck went on, 'but he's dreamed up an idea to get quick money and that's what we want. That's why I'm going along with him, but once we get the money ... this two thousand five hundred bucks ... we're going to ditch him.'

Meg's mind went back to her home. Suddenly and vividly, she saw her mother and father sitting in the shabby little living-room watching the lighted screen of the television set. She could see her mother's shapeless body slumped in the armchair. Her father had the habit of lifting his dentures with his tongue and settling them back into place with a distinct click. Her mother always kicked off her shoes when watching the telly: her feet were big and studded with corns.

'Baby!'

Chuck's voice snapped her back into the dreary room with its damp stains on the walls and the noise from the quay drifting up through the open window.

'I'm listening.'

'As soon as we've collected the money,' Chuck said, 'we'll take his car and beat it. There's nothing he can do! Two thousand five hundred bucks!'

She remembered what he had said:

When you get stuck with a crazy Indian, you're stuck with something special. Okay, so suppose you get as far as Miami? What's the good of getting to Miami if you land up with a knife in your guts or a slug in your head?

It was at this moment she ceased to care about death, pain, the police or anything.

What did it matter? What the hell did anything matter?

The lobby of the Excelsior hotel was crowded with tourists waiting with the patience of sheep for the bus to arrive to take them to yet another dismal hotel with another high sounding name.

None of the tourists looked at Meg as she crossed to the line

102

of telephone booths. Booth No. 3 was unoccupied. She slid open the door, stepped in and felt under the coin box. The envelope, fastened by tape was there. She jerked it free and put it in her handbag. She made no pretence about faking a call. Precautions? She just didn't care any more.

She walked out of the hotel and across the boulevard, feeling the sun hot on her face.

She got into the Buick, opened her bag and dropped the envelope on Chuck's knees.

'No trouble?'

She saw he was looking towards the hotel. She saw his small eyes were darting like the eyes of a trapped rat. He cared, she thought. He was frightened while she had lost all feeling of fear. That put her one up on him and she felt a small surge of triumph.

She watched him rip open the envelope, count the money and heard him suck in a quick breath. Watching him, seeing the fear, the greed, the immaturity on the suntanned face, the hopelessness of her future with him swept over her like a shroud drawn quickly over a dead face.

'Now the railroad station,' Chuck said. 'Telephone booth 8. I can't park there. I'll drive around and pick you up.'

He drove down side streets to avoid the heavy traffic of the boulevard while Meg sat still, her hands between her knees, looking sightlessly through the dusty windshield of the car.

'Okay, baby!'

Her thoughts were miles away and it wasn't until Chuck shook her arm roughly that she came out of her trance: a trance in the safety of the past.

She went into the station, moved through the crowds and to Booth 8 of a line of telephone booths. She collected the envelope, stuck under the coin box, then putting it into her bag, she walked to the station entrance and stood, waiting.

A minute or so later, the Buick slowed and she got in and Chuck drove away.

'No trouble?'

She again looked at his sweating face and darting eyes.

'No.'

He whistled softly.

'Man! This is like picking cherries.'

He drove until he found a parking bay, then he pulled up.

'Give.'

She handed him the envelope and while he slit it open, she watched the glossy, expensive cars drift by. She looked at the well fed faces: the women in their awful hats and the men with spider webs of broken veins covering their faces. People, she thought, who have security. Is this what security means: big cars, gross bodies, purple faces and flowered hats?

'We're a thousand bucks ahead,' Chuck said as he put the envelope in the glove compartment. 'You see what I said ... a gold plated meal ticket?'

She nodded, scarcely hearing what he was saying.

From his pocket he took a scrap of paper that he had found in the bottom of the sack of oranges Poke had given him.

'Here we go ... the Adlon hotel. Booth 4.' He set the car in motion. 'The Adlon? That's third right, isn't it?'

'I don't know.'

'Do you know anything?' Chuck snarled. 'Do I have to do all the goddamn thinking?'

Ten minutes later, Meg came out of the Adlon hotel and waited until the Buick pulled up. She got in and Chuck, his eyes darting uneasily, drove away.

'No trouble?'

'No.'

'This coon really has a bright idea!' Chuck said and steering the car into another parking bay, he pulled up and slit open the envelope.

'One thousand five hundred,' he muttered. 'Two more, then we take off.' He checked the list. 'The airport this time. Booth C. Then the Greyhound bus station. Booth 6.'

Chuck found parking near the entrance to the airport.

'Hurry it up, baby,' he said. 'I'll wait here.'

She walked quickly across the tarmac and into the busy lobby of the airport. She didn't give a damn if anyone was watching her or not. She went to the line of telephone booths. A man was just coming out of Booth C. He glanced at her and she saw disapproval in his eyes. He was middle-aged with a neat pot belly and immaculately dressed. The kind of square she hated. She brushed by him and entered the booth. She didn't even bother to close the door nor look around to see if the man was watching her.

She put her fingers under the coin box and felt metal. She stiffened, then felt again. There was no envelope under the box!

She looked hastily over her shoulder at the glass door. She had made no mistake. This was Booth C.

'Are you going to use the phone or are you sheltering from the rain?' a man asked sarcastically.

Another sleekily dressed, pot bellied square, she thought as she left the booth. God! how she hated these successful bastards with their smug, know-all expressions!

She walked quickly back to the parked Buick and got in.

'Okay?' Chuck asked as he started the engine.

'No.'

His hand hovered over the gearstick.

'What do you mean . . . no?'

'You said Booth C?'

'Yes . . . you heard what I said!'

'There was nothing there.'

Chuck's face turned vicious.

'Are you trying to gyp me, you stupid bitch?'

She dropped her handbag on his knees.

'Take a look. Go in there and see for yourself. There's nothing in Booth C.'

Chuck shoved the handbag back to her.

'You go back and check every booth! There could be a mistake.'

'You do it.'

He slammed his fist down on her knee. Pain shot right through her. She hunched forward, her hands gripping her knee.

'Get in there and check!' he snarled.

She got out of the car and returned to the airport lobby. Her knee hurt so badly she limped. Most of the telephone booths were occupied. Now, she didn't give a damn what happened to her.

She opened the booth door whether anyone was using the booth or not, pushed the caller aside, felt under the coin box, then went on to the next booth. There was something about her white face and her staring eyes that silenced any protest.

It took her less than five minutes to go through all the booths and to make sure there was no envelope under any of the coin boxes. By now people were staring at her.

A large man wearing a tweed hat, with a cigar clamped between his teeth was in the last booth. He pressed back against the wall of the booth as Meg leaned forward to feel under the coin box.

'You lost something, chick?' he said with a wide grin.

'Not you, freak,' she said and turning, she hurried back to the Buick.

'Nothing,' she said as she got into the car.

'Hell! What's gone wrong? Do you think some funk found it before you got there?'

Meg rubbed her knee which was still aching.

'I don't know.'

'Is that all you can say?' Chuck snarled. 'Five hundred bucks!'

He drove away from the airport and headed for the Greyhound bus station. During the drive he kept muttering to himself and every now and then he would pound his clenched fist on the driving wheel.

'You don't give a damn, do you?' he said. 'You stupid, zombie bitch!'

Meg said nothing. She leaned back in the seat, rubbing her aching knee, her eyes lost.

At the Greyhound bus station, Chuck saw it was impossible to park. He slowed and leaning across Meg, he opened the off side door.

'Booth 6 . . . get going. I'll be back.'

Meg got out of the car and walked into the crowded lobby as Chuck pulled away.

A girl was using Booth 6 and Meg saw that she would have to wait. This girl had a face carved out of stone. She had long blonde hair and finger nails like claws. She was wearing expensive clothes and as she talked, she waved her hand that carried three diamond rings.

The girl continued to talk while Meg watched her. But after a while, she became aware of Meg and her hand began to wave less.

There was something about Meg's stillness, her dirty sweater, her stained hipsters and her lank long hair that upset the girl's concentration. Finally, she hung up, left the booth, making a circle as she passed Meg.

Meg went into the booth and into the smell of expensive perfume. She found an envelope under the coin box and she came out of the booth.

A young man in a turtle neck yellow sweater and white slacks, his long hair flopping on his collar, his sideboards making points to his chin, smiled at her.

'Treasure hunt?' he asked.

At one time a boy like this would have thrilled her. Now, she saw him only as a sex symbol and trouble.

She stared stonily at him and then went past him. She knew a man like this: clean, well off, romantic, handsome was lost to her. Walking away from him, to her, was like dying.

She gave the envelope to Chuck who opened it and checked that here were five one hundred dollar bills in the envelope.

'Two thousand,' he muttered, then thought for a long moment. He put the envelope in the glove compartment. 'It'll have to do. We're getting out of here, baby. Two thousand is better than nothing. We'll go back, pick up our things, then we'll head for Los Angeles.'

While he drove to Paradise City, Meg stared out of the window, looking at the traffic, then at the bathers as they had fun on the beach, then at the fruit stalls as they reached the waterfront.

Chuck took the envelopes from the glove compartment and put them inside his shirt.

'Come on ... let's get packed,' he said. There was a nervous note in his voice. He looked at his watch. The time was 12.45. It had been a long morning. In another half hour, they would be heading along highway 25: Belle Glade, Whidden, Buckingham, Nocatte, then onto highway 17.

Two thousand dollars was better than nothing!

They walked along the quay, down the smelly alley and to their rooming house.

The fat Indian was behind his desk. He beamed at them as they went past him and climbed the stairs to their room.

Two thousand dollars! Chuck was thinking as he followed her, plus the car. This crazy Indian wouldn't dare squeal to the police about losing his car. Once they were on the road, they were shot of him and with two thousand dollars!

Meg paused on the landing.

'Well, go on ... go on!' Chuck said irritably and stepping around her, he opened the door of their room.

Poke Toholo was sitting on the bed, eating an orange. As Chuck came to a standstill in the doorway, Poke spat an orange pip on to the floor.

'How much did you get?' he asked, his black eyes glittering.

*

107

It was while Meg was at the Greyhound bus station waiting for the girl with the diamond rings to finish her telephone conversation that Captain Terrell finally decided that an Indian called Poke Toholo was the Executioner.

Laying the last report he had been reading down on his desk, he pushed back his chair and lit his pipe.

'He's our boy,' he said to Beigler. 'Now we've got to find him.'

The report from the Homicide squad had made the decision final. The squad not only had found in the cabin of the Welcome motel Poke's finger prints that matched the prints they had found in the small back room where Poke had lived with his parents, but they had also found the unmistakable signs that a gun had been hidden under the mattress in the motel cabin. There was not only the imprint still to be seen in the floppy mattress but also gun oil.

To add to this, Poke's description Mrs. Bertha Harris had given them matched the description Lepski had got from Dr. Wanniki.

Dr. Wanniki was over eighty years of age and his eyesight was failing. Lepski got the impression that the doctor's mind could also be failing. For minor ailments he was still in the running and the Seminole Indians went to him because their grandparents had gone to him.

'Poke isn't a bad boy,' Wanniki told Lepski. 'A little quick tempered perhaps, but then the young are quick tempered. Mentally sick?' The old man stroked his bristly chin. He had forgotten to shave that morning. 'Well, there are many people mentally sick. I wouldn't say Poke ...' He broke off and stared at Lepski uneasily as if a thought had struck him: a thought that hadn't occurred to him before. 'He did have a quick temper.'

Lepski questioned and probed but he couldn't get anything else from the old man except a description that matched that of the man who had stayed at the Welcome motel.

'Well, we now know who he is,' Terrell said. 'The motive beats me. Can it be possible this man killed all these people because an old woman called him a nigger?'

'He's a nutter,' Beigler said. 'He's got a blood lust. He's making the rich sweat. You never know what triggers off a nut.'

'Now we've got to find him.'

'Yeah.' Beigler had been doing his homework. 'There are one hundred and fifty two Seminole Indians registered in the

City,' he said, 'and half of them look alike. The other half look like the other half except they are older. We'd better put out we want to talk to Poke Toholo: get it on the radio and TV and the press. Do you think the Mayor would offer a reward? That could flush Toholo out if the reward was big enough.'

Terrell considered this.

'These Indians stick together. Up to now this man doesn't know we're on to him.' He paused to light his pipe. 'Once he does know he'll go underground. I have the idea that right now he is feeling safe enough to be in the open, but once he goes into hiding, it could be one hell of a job to find him.'

'Not if the reward is big enough,' Beigler said who believed in the power of money.

'Our boys have been working non-stop for the past days checking on the Indians. What have they come up with?'

'Enough paper to sink a battleship.'

'What have you done with it?'

'Turned the lot over to Jack Hatchee.'

Terrell squinted at Beigler through his pipe smoke.

'That's a bright idea, Joe.'

'I get them from time to time,' Beigler said not without a touch of smugness. 'If Jack can't make sense out of these reports no one can.'

Jack Hatchee was the only Seminole Indian on the City's police force. He worked in Records and he was elderly and known for a long memory.

'See if he's got anything yet.'

Beigler shook his head.

'He'll tell us, Chief. He's got a ton of paper to wade through and he's not anyone you can hurry. Best leave him alone. I told him it was urgent.'

Terrell sucked at his pipe. He thought for a long moment, then pawed through the reports on his desk until he came up with two sheets of paper. He studied them while Beigler lit a cigarette.

'We'll wait to see if Jack comes up with something,' he said finally. 'I'm sure if we give out we're after Toholo a smoke screen will come down and we won't find him.' He tapped the report he was holding with the stem of his pipe. 'But we have these other two: Mr. and Mrs. Jack Allen. We know Poke had someone working with him. According to this Mrs. Harris, a man and a woman arrived with Poke at the motel. It's a safe bet these two are the ones helping Poke. We have descriptions of them and a description of their car. So, Joe, we go after them. When we pick them up, they'll lead us to Poke. Get the boys working on it.' He handed the two sheets of paper to Beigler. 'They'll be staying somewhere. Check every cheap hotel, rooming house and look for the Buick. Once we've found them, we'll find Poke.'

The intercom on the desk buzzed. Terrell flicked down a switch.

'Chief?'

It was Sergeant Tanner.

'What is it, Charlie?'

'I have a lady here ... says she wants to talk to you. Mrs. Matilda Dobey. I told her you were busy but she says she is too and its important.'

'Did you ask what it's about?'

'Yeah ... she says it's not my business,' Tanner said, his voice sour.

Terrell hesitated, then shrugged.

'Okay ... send her up.'

He looked at Beigler.

'Does Mrs Matilda Dobey mean anything to you, Joe?'

'If it did, I wouldn't admit it,' Beigler said and got to his feet. 'I'll get the boys working.'

He left the office and made for the Detectives' room.

A few minutes later, Sergeant Tanner knocked on Terrell's door, then looked in.

'Mrs. Dobey, Chief.'

Terrell pushed aside the pile of papers on his desk and said in a resigned voice, 'Show her in, Charlie.'

Mrs. Matilda Dobey was a tiny woman in her late seventies. She was dressed neatly but shabbily in black. She had snow white hair and very alert blue eyes.

'Are you Chief of Police?' she demanded, coming to rest before Terrell's desk.

Terrell got to his feet and gave her his warm, friendly smile.

'That's right, Mrs. Dobey.'

He came around his desk to pull up a chair.

Mrs. Dobey regarded him with approval.

'Thank you. I'm not as young as I used to be, but I don't consider myself yet as old.'

'Would you like a cup of coffee, Mrs. Dobey?' Terrell asked as he went back to his chair and sat down.

'No, thank you. I have things to do. I may tell you I've come a long way out of my way. I'm due back to get Mr. Dobey his dinner. He'll be worrying about me.'

'What's the trouble?' Terrell asked, laying his big hands on the mass of papers on his desk.

'I have just come from the airport. I was seeing my grandson off. I wanted to telephone my daughter to tell her Jerry ... that's my grandson ... had got off all right.' Mrs. Dobey paused. 'I don't want you to imagine I'm talking for the sake of talking, but I know when one talks to police officers one has to give facts ... that's right, isn't it?'

'That's right,' Terrell said. His virtue was patience and this was one of the reasons why he was a good Chief of Police.

'My daughter has a job in an office. My sister who lives in Miami is taking care of Jerry ... but, that won't interest you. I agreed to see Jerry off because my daughter was tied up with this office ... that's what grandmas are for, aren't they?'

Terrell sucked at his pipe and nodded.

'I guess that's right, Mrs. Dobey.'

'My daughter takes it for granted, but young people do take things for granted. I don't mind. Don't think I'm complaining.'

Terrell tapped ashes out of his pipe.

'You telephoned your daughter?' he said as he began to refill his pipe.

'Yes. I went into one of the booths at the airport. I happened to drop my purse.' She looked at Terrell, her alert eyes quizzing. 'Call it old age if you like, but it could have happened to anyone.'

'Yes, I guess so,' Terrell said. 'I'm always dropping things myself.'

Mrs. Dobey looked at him suspiciously.

'You don't have to say that to be polite.'

'You dropped your purse?'

She smiled; it was a nice understanding smile.

'The trouble with me, Chief, is I talk too much. Excuse me.' She settled herself more comfortably in her chair, then went on, 'When I bent to pick up my purse I saw this envelope under the coin box ... stuck there with tape.' She opened her large, shabby handbag and took out an envelope. 'Now that, I thought, is a very funny place for an envelope to be.' She looked

111

directly at Terrell. 'I've probably done wrong, but I opened it. But if I hadn't opened it, how would I know what was inside? Perhaps I should have gone to the first police officer I saw and given it to him without opening it. Should I have done that?'

'What's inside the envelope?' Terrell asked, avoiding the question.

'A lot of money ... a lot of money.' She regarded him. 'As soon as I looked inside and saw all this money I knew I shouldn't have opened it. I knew I had to come to you and not give it to any police officer. So much money offers a temptation and police officers aren't millionaires.'

Terrell cleared his throat.

'May I have the envelope, Mrs. Dobey? I'll give you a receipt for it.'

'I don't want a receipt,' she said, handing over the envelope. 'I just want to get home so I can get Mr. Dobey his dinner.'

Seven

Poke Toholo dropped the half eaten orange on the floor and kicked it under the bed. He wiped his fingers on his hipsters, then held out his hand.

'How much did you get?' he asked.

Chuck came into the room as if he knew the floor was full of dry rot and would cave in under his weight.

His mind was paralysed at the sight of the Indian sitting on the bed. Ten seconds ago, he was imagining himself in the car with Meg at his side, with two thousand dollars in his pocket. This sudden spin of the coin sealed his reflexes as if the nerve cells in his brain had been cut.

'How much did you get?' Poke repeated.

Chuck pulled himself together and part of his brain began to function.

Did this crazy Indian suspect anything? he asked himself.

He looked at Poke, seeing the expressionless brown face and the glittering black eyes, but there was nothing to tell him that Poke suspected he had been about to be betrayed.

112

'One of them didn't pay up,' Chuck said huskily.

He became aware that Meg was behind him so he moved further into the room so she could come in.

She went over to the window, not looking at Poke and sat down on the only upright chair, lifting her hair off her shoulders and letting it drop back in an indifferent movement that made Chuck want to hit her. She leaned forward, her elbows resting on the window ledge and stared down at the busy quay.

'Do you expect me to believe that?' Poke asked, staring at Chuck.

Chuck moistened his lips with his tongue.

'Ask her . . . she collected the envelopes.'

'I'm asking you,' Poke said.

Slowly and reluctantly Chuck took the four envelopes from inside his shirt. They were damp with his sweat and he tossed them on the bed.

'One of them didn't pay up . . . the one at the airport: I sent her back. She checked every booth.'

'The airport!' Poke's face relaxed. 'Hansen . . . yes . . . I go along with that. Hansen wouldn't pay, but he will.'

Chuck didn't know what he was talking about. He leaned against the wall, trying to make himself relax. He watched Poke open the envelopes and count the money. Poke flicked six one hundred dollar bills in Chuck's direction.

'Five more tomorrow,' Poke said. He produced a slip of paper which he dropped on the bed. 'Like milking a cow, isn't it?'

'Yeah.' Chuck watched the Indian put the rest of the money in his pocket. 'That's it . . . yeah.'

Poke got to his feet and moved past Chuck to the door.

'They may not all pay, but most of them will.' His black eyes stared fixedly at Chuck. 'They're scared. When people get scared they do what they're told,' and he was gone.

There was a long pause, then Meg said without looking around, 'Do you want me to pack?'

'Didn't you hear what he said, you dumb bitch?' Chuck snarled. 'We do it again tomorrow.'

'Do we?'

There was a note in her voice that made him look sharply at her. She still continued to look out of the window. Her hair hid her face, but the note in her voice made him uneasy. He suddenly realised he would never have the nerve to go to those booths and pick up the money. He could never bring himself to do it. It was a goddamn trap. The thought of the cops descending on him as he took the envelope from its hiding place made him sweat.

He picked up the piece of paper Poke had left and read what was written there:

Airport Booth B.

Greyhound Bus. Booth 4.

Railroad station. Booth 1.

Excelsior Booth 2.

Adlon Booth 6.

Okay, he thought, suppose only three of them jelled: fifteen hundred dollars plus the six hundred Poke had given him! But this time he wouldn't return to this dump. As soon as they picked up the last envelope they would go. He had been crazy to have come back this time to pick up their things.

'Listen,' he said, 'tomorrow, we get the money and we go. This time we don't come back. That's where I went wrong. Tomorrow, as soon as we've got the money, we drive off. He won't know about it until we're miles away.'

She turned and looked at him.

'You aren't much, are you, Chuck?' she said quietly. 'I thought you were somebody. I guess I'm stupid. I've got nothing now. I've got less than nothing.'

'You're going to share two thousand dollars with me, you dope! Is that less than nothing?' Chuck demanded angrily. 'Tomorrow, we'll be in the clear. You're going to do it, aren't you?'

She turned and looked out of the window. The sponge boats were coming in. Three men were struggling with a hundred pound turtle. The Indians were waving oranges and yelling at indifferent buyers.

Chuck got to his feet and went over to her. He pulled her away from the window. His hot, sweaty hands gripped her arms and he shook her.

'You're going to do it, aren't you?' he demanded.

'I'll do it,' she said and the lost look in her eyes made Chuck release her. 'Why should I care, you gold plated meal ticket?'

While she was speaking, Poke had come to rest before the desk of the fat, smiling Indian who owned the rooming house.

This Indian's name was Ocida. His fat, simple face hid a criminal mind. The rooming house was a cover for his many activities. He was a man of considerable substance. He had a

Swiss bank account. He was the head of a L.S.D. smuggling ring. He controlled twenty-six Indian prostitutes who paid him a quarter of their earnings. He had a 2% cut on all the fruit sold in the markets because he had made a deal with a Mafia Union man. He had a 1% cut on the turtle soup industry because a number of Indians worked in the turtle factories and he controlled most of the Indian labour. He had a 3% cut on all parking fees on the quay because, until he got his cut, cars got pushed into the harbour.

Ocida was the hidden man behind most of the rackets on the quay and he was smart enough to keep hidden.

He was happy to sit behind the desk in this shabby rooming house, smiling, picking his teeth and making sums in his head. People worked for him. Money flowed in. Why should he worry? Money moved from Paradise City to Berne, Switzerland. Money to him was like a Picasso painting to an art lover. You had it, you kept it, you admired it and you were happy.

Ocida liked Poke Toholo. He knew he was dangerous, but if you were going to make a living out of this stupid, sloppy world, you had to be dangerous.

He knew Poke was the Executioner as he knew everything criminal in the City. He considered this idea to get even with the rich whites was inventive. He admired any form of invention. He knew too that Poke was a little sick in the head. Well, lots of people did important things who were sick in the head. Any man, sick or not, who could dream up an idea to scare the rich whites and make money out of it, had Ocida's approval.

So when Poke came to rest before Ocida's desk, Ocida turned on his widest smile.

'I want a gun,' Poke said softly.

Ocida leaned forward and selected a quill toothpick from a box on the far side of his desk. He inserted the quill between two of his gold capped molars while he regarded Poke.

'What kind of gun?' he asked.

'A good one . . . .38, automatic and accurate,' Poke told him.

Ocida removed the quill, wiped what was on it on his shirt sleeve, then put the quill back in the box.

'Guns cost money, Poke. Have you money?'

'I'll pay a hundred dollars.'

Ocida admired men who didn't fear him. Poke was one of the very few.

'Wait.'

He left his desk and heaved his bulk into the back room. Some ten minutes later, he returned with a parcel done up in brown paper and tied with string. He put the parcel on his desk.

As Poke felt in his hip pocket, Ocida shook his head.

'It cost me nothing . . . so why should it cost you anything?'

Poke put a one hundred dollar bill on the desk and picked up the parcel.

'I pay for what I want,' he said curtly and walked out into the hot sunshine.

Ocida lost his habitual smile. He stared at the bill, then put it in his shirt pocket.

He believed no one should ever part with money unless he had to. This was his philosophy of life.

He rubbed the side of his fat jaw.

Maybe this boy was sicker than he had thought.

*

As Beigler handed back the extortion note to Terrell, he said, 'Well, now we know the motive.'

'It had to be more than an old woman calling him a nigger,' Terrell said. 'How many other members of the Fifty Club have had the same demand? You follow my thinking? These people at the club, scared sick by what has already happened, could be getting demands for money and to save their skins, could be paying up and not reporting to us.

Beigler lit another cigarette.

'I can't say I blame them, Chief. It's a smart ploy if that's his racket. Three of them have been knocked off to soften the others up and we haven't done much to give the rest of the old dears much confidence, have we?'

Terrell nodded.

'I'll see Hansen. We'll have to give him protection and I mean protection. He paid up, but Poke hasn't had the money and he might think Hansen didn't pay and he could hit back. Get a couple of good men guarding the front and back of the club. Every Indian going in and out is to be checked.'

Beigler went off to the Detectives' room while Terrell went down the back stairs to the police yard where his car was parked.

The Detectives' room was deserted when Beigler walked in. Every available man was out trying to find a couple who called themselves Mr. and Mrs. Jack Allen. Realising the urgency to get Hansen guarded, Beigler reluctantly called Captain Hemmings of the Miami police force to ask for additional help.

116

'You've already got fifteen of my men,' Hemmings pointed out. 'Do you imagine we haven't any crime in our own City?'

'If I could borrow two more men, sir,' Beigler said, 'I'd be obliged. I'll send them back the moment I have two of my own boys available.'

'You know something, Joe? If I was handling this thing of yours, I'd have this Redskin in the tank by now. Frank's handling it all wrong, but it's his territory so who am I to talk?'

Beigler controlled his temper with an effort.

'Captain Terrell knows what he is doing, sir.'

The strangled note in Beigler's voice reminded Hemmings that he was criticising Beigler's boss.

'Sure,' he said hastily. 'Well, okay. I'll get a couple of men over to you. Maybe if we ever have a crime wave here, you'll help us, huh?' He gave a short barking laugh. 'If we ever need help which we won't.'

'I hope not, sir.' Beigler would have liked to have been able to slide along the telephone line, kick Hemmings' fat rear and slide back to safety to his desk, but miracles don't happen that way.

'Your man will be covered in an hour,' Hemmings promised.

But this coverage came to late. While Terrell was snarled up in the heavy traffic and while Hemmings was detailing two detectives to get over to Paradise City, Poke Toholo struck.

Killing Elliot Hansen didn't present any difficulties. There were risks, of course, but Poke was ready to accept risks.

The time was 14.30: the time when the Club lunch was over; when the Indian staff were in the vast kitchen in the basement having their own lunch; when two-thirds of the members of the Club had gone back to their offices and the other third were snoozing in the lounge. All this Poke knew. He also knew at this time Elliot Hansen retired to his office and stretched himself out in a couch for a forty minute nap. Because Hansen had sensitive nerves, at his own expense, he had had this office sound proofed. This Poke also knew.

He arrived at the staff entrance of the Club about the same time two bored detectives were heading for Paradise City and at the same time as Captain Terrell pulled up before a red traffic light, some half a mile from the Club.

Poke moved silently along the dim corridor, listening to the noise the staff made as they ate and talked in the kitchen. He took from a rack one of the many white coats hanging there

117

and put it on. It was a little too big for him, but this didn't matter. He walked past the open kitchen door and no one noticed him. He moved into the deserted dining-room, then into the corridor and along to the bar. He slowed his step as he reached the entrance to the bar. He saw his father washing used glasses with that patience and servility that always angered Poke. He paused just out of sight to take a long look at the old man and he felt the urge to go into the big room and take his father in his arms. He knew he couldn't afford such a luxury and he moved on.

Two club members: sleek, well fed men with cigars between their fingers went by him. They didn't see him. Who saw a monkey in a white coat? He was as anonymous as a fly on the wall.

He reached Hansen's office. He didn't even look around to see if anyone was watching. He turned the handle gently and moved into the room. The door closed with a soft sigh as the air was expelled by the sound proofing around the door.

Elliot Hansen was sitting at his desk. Usually at this time, he would be asleep, but now he was too frightened to sleep. The world he had built up was crumbling and soon, he felt, it would crash down on him.

He looked up and saw an Indian in a white jacket and he waved impatiently.

'I didn't ring for you! Go away! What do you mean coming in . . .' Then he recognised Poke and with a shuddering gasp, he shrank back in his chair.

Poke lifted the gun. There was a little smile on his brown face as he squeezed the trigger.

The first bullet made a blossom of blood on Hansen's white jacket at his right shoulder that told Poke the gun threw to the right. The second bullet hit Hansen in the mouth, smashing his beautiful white dentures. The third bullet scattered his brains on his blotter.

That was the way Captain Terrell found him when he arrived ten minutes later.

*

Sergeant Beigler had sweat beads on his face and a stormy look in his eyes when he came into Terrell's office. Terrell had handed him the thankless task of handling the press, instructing him to give out no information. The reaction of the press to this was almost too much for Beigler's blood pressure.

'Do you know what those sonsofbitches are calling us?' he said, clenching and unclenching his big fists. 'The Keystone cops! They said . . .'

'All right, Joe, never mind about them.' Terrell had just had a session on the telephone with Mayor Hedley who was almost hysterical. When Terrell was sure he was playing his cards right no amount of hysteria nor shouting could ruffle him. 'Sit down . . . have some coffee.'

Beigler sat down and poured coffee that had just arrived into a paper cup.

'We're in for a hell of a press tomorrow, Chief,' he said, trying to calm down. 'And tonight on TV news . . . that'll be something!'

'You told them we had no leads?'

Beigler winced at the memory.

'I told them.'

Terrell began to fill his pipe.

'Good. How many men have you pulled in?'

'Six waiting outside.'

'Let's have them in.'

Headed by Lepski, five of Terrell's best men came into the office. There was Max Jacoby, Dave Farrell, Jack Wallace, Andy Shields and Alec Horn.

'Find chairs,' Terrell said, 'and sit down.'

After a few moments of confusion the six detectives got themselves seated.

'You know the situation,' Terrell said. 'You've all read the reports. Our number one is Poke Toholo. These two who call themselves Mr. and Mrs. Jack Allen are working with him and could lead us to him. You have their descriptions. They shouldn't be difficult to spot because they don't know we are on to them. This is why we're taking a beating from the press. We've given out we haven't any lead and as long as the press call us the Keystone Cops the more relaxed these three will be and that's what I want them to be . . . relaxed.' He paused to light his pipe, then went on, 'I am sure a number of the members of the Fifty Club have had demands for money and I'm equally sure they have paid up, but none of them will admit it. They are a spinelesss lot and Hansen's killing has scared them witless. Hansen did pay, but someone found the money before Poke did, so he killed Hansen. The idea of taping an envelope with money in it under the coin box of a public telephone is a smart one. Public telephones are continually in use and it would be almost impossible to spot anyone collecting the envelope if it were not for the fact that we have the descriptions of these three: this they don't know and they mustn't know. We know they have used a telephone booth at the airport and as they don't know we're on to them, they could use it again. Max, Dave and Jack, you go down to the airport right away. Go into each telephone booth and feel under the coin boxes. If you find an envelope, leave it where it is and call me. This is going to take a little time. You must act like anyone going into a telephone booth. Just remember you may be watched and one wrong move could bitch up this operation. I don't have to spell it out to you, do I?'

The three men nodded.

'If when you're there you spot any of these three, stick with them. You'll be in radio communication with Lepski. We want to pick them all up. If you spot the three together, then close in on them, but be careful ... they are dangerous. It's my bet only one of them will do the collecting ... probably the girl. If it's only one of them, tail her or him and keep reporting. Do you get all that?'

Again the three men nodded.

'Okay, get going.'

It was Jack Wallace who found the envelope under the coin box in Booth B in the airport lobby. He felt a little thrill of excitement as, leaning against the coin box, his big body blocking any watching eyes, his left hand went under the coin box as he dialled a number with his right. He had intended to have a quick word with his wife, but when he felt the envelope, he cut the connection and re-dialled, this time calling Terrell.

'I've found it, Chief,' he said. 'Booth B.'

Terrell drew in a long breath: his gamble had paid off!

'Fine, Jack. Leave the airport and report to Lepski.'

Wallace hung up and left the booth, glancing at the elderly woman who was impatiently waiting to take his place.

Lepski was sitting in his car, his radio switched on when Terrell's voice brought him to attention.

'Jack's found the envelope in Booth B,' Terrell told him. 'Take over, Tom; the operation is all yours ... and good luck.'

Lepski put his hand inside his jacket and touched the butt of his .38 police special as he said, 'Okay, Chief, I'll report when something happens,' and he switched off.

Wallace appeared by Lepski's car.

'Alert the others, Jack,' Lepski said. 'I'll go inside and take a look around.'

He left the car and walked across the vast parking lot into the airport lobby. He moved casually, edging his way through the loitering crowd. He passed the line of telephone booths, looked briefly at the elderly woman who was in Booth B, then went up the stairs leading to the gallery overlooking the lobby where the control offices were. Up on the gallery he had a clear view of Booth B.

'I'm sorry, sir,' a girl said, 'but you can't remain here. This is for the airport officials only.'

Lepski turned and eyed her.

She was small, pretty and dark, wearing the yellow blouse and the black mini skirt uniform of the Paradise City Airlines. For a long moment, his eyes dwelt on her legs, then as she gave an embarrassed giggle, he became all cop.

'Who's in charge up here?' he asked and showed his badge.

Minutes later, he was sitting in an office, looking through the glass partition down into the lobby and at Booth B, out of sight, and with his radio switched on.

Lepski was trained to wait. That was police business. The first four hours crawled by. At the end of each hour, one of his men went into the telephone booth to check the envelope was still there. Fifty-three people used the booth during the wait. For something better to do, Lepski counted them, but none of them matched the description of the three he was waiting for. After five hours, Max Jacoby relieved him and Lepski took a nap on a truckle bed lent by the Airport supervisor.

He dreamed of the air hostess. Her antics in his dream surprised him, and it took a lot to surprise him. He was a disillusioned man when he woke.

*

The first thing Chuck did after his morning coffee was to check the Buick. He drove the car to a service station, had the tank filled, had the tyres and battery checked and the radiator topped up. The garage hand told him two of the plugs should be replaced so Chuck had them replaced. Once he had collected the money, he had a long drive ahead of him and nothing must be left to chance. This was the end of the operation. To him, two thousand dollars and a car meant a new life. His mind was too narrow to wonder what would happen when the money was spent. He lived for the day. There was always more money to be found: always some paying racket if you looked for it. Why worry about tomorrow?

Satisfied the car was now in as perfect working order as it ever would be, he drove it to the waterfront and parked it. He checked his watch: the time was 10.43. In another half hour they would start the operation. Standing in the sun, he studied the paper Poke had given him. He decided to leave the airport to the last. From the airport he could drive to highway 25 and then away to Los Angeles. So the first stop would be the Adlon hotel.

He had told Meg who he had left in bed, to meet him on the waterfront. Lighting a cigarette, he walked over to a bollard and sat on it. This side of the harbour was empty. The sponge boats were at sea. On the other side of the harbour he could see the yachts, the motorboats and the sailing boats of the rich. He flicked ash into the oily water and rubbed his blunt nose with the back of his hand and tried to relax.

Chuck never read a newspaper nor listened to the radio. He lived in his own small, restricted world. So he knew nothing about Hansen's murder nor the subsequent uproar in the press.

Like milking a cow, Poke had said.

Chuck grinned uneasily. Not quite, but nearly. The cow could be dangerous. He wondered how the Indian would react when he found out he was the cow who was being milked.

A little after 11.00 he wandered back to the car.

At this hour of the day the quay was crowded with Indians, fishermen, tourists with their cameras and the crews off the luxury yachts. People were going into the bars for their first drink of the day. There was a crowd of tourists on the edge of the quay watching a lobster boat unload.

Meg came through the crowd and slid into the passenger's seat in the Buick. She was wearing her grubby white sweater and her worn hipsters; her long, lank hair flopped on her shoulders as she settled herself.

Chuck got under the wheel. He turned the ignition key and started the engine.

'This is it, baby,' he said. He tried to make his voice sound confident but he was uneasy. The next two hours could be dangerous. He wondered if Poke was at the fruit stall. He looked uneasily up and down the crowded quay.

As Meg said nothing, he looked sharply at her. She seemed relaxed and he looked at her hands: no tremor and this angered him. She was too goddamn cool, he thought, and he realised she just didn't care. This was dangerous. When you don't care, you took risks. He felt a spasm of fear as he thought of the possibility of some cop pouncing on her.

'As soon as we get the money, we're off,' he said. 'We'll go to Los Angeles . . . that's fun City. With two thousand bucks, we'll have a ball.'

Still she said nothing. She was staring out of the car window, her face blank and he had a vicious urge to hurt her, but this wasn't the time.

He thought back on the previous night. He had wanted and needed her. She had lain under him like a dead body. Nothing he had done to her had aroused her and when finally his lust had drained out of him, he had rolled off her in disgust.

As he shifted into reverse to back the car out of the parking bay, he suddenly decided he had had enough of her. He would ditch her as he was ditching the Indian. As soon as she had collected all the envelopes and they were on highway 27, he would stop and throw her out. With two thousand dollars or whatever they collected, he was sure he could find a girl who wouldn't react to him like this goddamn zombie. *Less than nothing*! Wasn't that what she had said about him? Okay, he would lose her, but not until she had got the envelopes!

'We go to the Adlon first,' he said. 'Booth 6. Are you listening?'

'Yes,' Meg said.

As he edged the car along the crowded quay and up a side street that would bring them to the main boulevard, Patrol Officer O'Grady was standing at the street corner leading to the boulevard.

Every patrolman had had his instructions and a description. The instructions had been emphatic: *don't arrest, report*. He eyed the dusty Buick and came alert. As the car crawled past him he looked at Chuck and then at Meg and instantly recognised them from the description he had learned by heart. The temptation to stop the car and make the arrest was almost too much for him. He imagined his photograph in all the papers and perhaps even giving a TV interview but the thought of

Beigler's wrath cooled the temptation. He watched the car join the heavy traffic on the boulevard, then switched on his two-way radio.

Waiting for his information, Beigler alerted Patrol car 4.

Police Officer Hurn with Police Officer Jason were parked on the boulevard. They came alert as Beigler's voice snapped out of the radio box.

'X.50. 1963 dark blue Buick. No 55789 heading your way. Repeat X.50. Tail if you can, but lose it if you think you could be spotted. Man and woman. Repeat leave them alone if there's any chance of them spotting you.'

The code signal X.50 told Hurn that this was the Executioner operation. He started the car engine. He kept his radio on and could hear Beigler alerting the other patrol cars.

'Here they come,' Jason said, and Hurn began to move the police car into the stream of traffic.

The Buick went past them and both officers got a good look at Chuck and Meg. Hurn forced his car between a Rolls and a Cadillac. The driver of the Rolls tapped his horn, then realised he was showing disapproval to a police car. He tried to look as if he had touched the horn button by accident as Jason glared at him.

The Buick beat the traffic lights ahead and Hurn cursed as he had to stop.

'We're bitched,' he said. 'The only way to get through this mess is to sound the siren. There they go. We've lost them.'

He reported back to Beigler.

Oblivious that they had been spotted, Chuck turned right at the next intersection and slowed as he reached the Adlon hotel.

'Go ahead, baby, I'll wait here.'

Meg went into the hotel and collected the envelope from Booth 6. She returned to the car and put the envelope in the glove compartment. From the Adlon hotel Chuck drove to the Excelsior hotel and again Meg collected an envelope without trouble.

With a growing feeling of elation, Chuck watched her put the envelope into the glove compartment, then he drove towards the City's railroad station.

'Man!' he muttered to himself, 'this really is like milking a cow! A thousand bucks ahead! Three more stops and we're home!'

Patrol car 6 reported that the Buick had passed them, going in the opposite direction. The traffic had been too heavy to turn so they had lost them.

Beigler looked at the large scale map spread out on his desk. He pin-pointed where the Buick had been seen and alerted Patrol cars 1 and 2 that the Buick could be heading their way.

But Chuck used the side streets to get to the railroad station and the Patrol cars missed him.

Chuck had to circle around the station as there was no parking space. This bothered him. Some nosey cop could stop him and ask him what he was waiting for. He had to circle the station four times before he saw Meg, waiting.

Sweat was running down his face as he pulled up.

'Krist! You've taken your goddamn time!' he snarled as she got into the car and he pulled away. 'Did you get it?'

'Yes.' Meg opened the glove compartment and put the third envelope on top of the other two.

'Phew!' Chuck wiped his face with the back of his hand. 'For a moment ...' He stopped and forced a grin. 'Fifteen hundred bucks! Now for the Greyhound!'

He cut down a side street and onto Seaview Boulevard. A Patrol officer, very much on his toes, spotted the Buick as it crawled with the heavy traffic and he alerted Beigler. Beigler alerted Patrol car 2 but this car was hopelessly snarled up in the traffic. The driv_r said there was nothing he could do about it unless he let loose with his siren. Beigler accepted this, cursing. It maddened him that the boulevard was choked with loafing drivers who were showing off their cars and themselves and watching the capers of the people on the beach.

Meg left the Buick and walked into the Greyhound bus station.

Booth 4 was occupied.

The young woman in her early thirties, using the telephone, was the type Meg hated and despised: married with a cheap hair-do, a dress not just good enough and junk costume jewellery. She would have spawned a child of course about whom she would talk incessantly, concealing the fact the child was a monster without discipline and made her life a misery. She would be married to a drag of a man who could only talk about money and golf and was scared witless of losing his job.

Hating her, Meg watched her as she talked, waving her hand

... yak ... yak ... yak. Her shrill laugh came through the dusty glass door. Yak ... yak ... yak.

Losing patience, Meg opened the booth door, shoved the woman aside, felt under the coin box, found the envelope, jerked it loose and put it in her bag.

'Well! Excuse me!' the woman said, her eyes popping wide open.

'Screw you,' Meg said, then walked away to where Chuck was waiting.

'No trouble?' Chuck said as Meg put the envelope into the glove compartment.

She looked stonily at him.

'Would I be here if there was?'

Chuck drew in a long breath.

Two thousand dollars!

'What's the matter with you?' he demanded as he drove onto the highway. 'Just what the hell's the matter with you?'

'I wish I knew,' Meg said. 'How I wish I knew!'

Well, he would soon be rid of her, Chuck told himself. She's as crazy as the Indian! But what did it matter so long as he was shot of them both? The airport the next stop! Even if there was no envelope waiting, he now had two thousand six hundred dollars! Man! Could you have a ball with that kind of bread!

They arrived at the airport as the hands of the big clock in the lobby showed 12.15.

Chuck found parking space among the many cars drawn up in orderly rows in the big parking lot. He could smell his own sweat as he yanked the pistol grip brake lever.

'Here we go, baby ... last round up! Come on ... come on, get moving!'

Meg got out of the car and started across the tarmac towards the airport.

Chuck checked to see there was no one near by, then taking the envelopes from the glove compartment, he slit them open with his knife. Money spilt out on his knees.

Milking a cow! Picking cherries! What a sweet racket!

Having counted the money, he put the bills into one envelope and balling the other three envelopes, he tossed them on the back seat. Then he put the heavily stuffed envelope in the glove compartment.

If this last one jelled, he would have three thousand one hundred dollars!

Man! Man! Man!

He thumped his fist on the steering wheel.

Come on! Come on! he thought. Come on, you zombie bitch! Let's get the hell out of here!

Then he thought of the moment when he would pull up on the highway, open the off-side door and throw her out.

He thought of her standing by the side of the highway, looking after him as he drove away.

Man! Would that be the moment!

*

Lepski had been on duty since 11.00. There was nothing to report so far, Jacoby had told him. The envelope was still in place. The other detectives had been relieved and were now back on the scene.

'We could wait here for weeks,' Lepski said sourly as he lit a cigarette and settled in the chair.

'I'm going to get a cup of coffee ... okay?' Jacoby made a move to the door.

Then Beigler's voice came in over the radio. The two men stiffened to attention.

Beigler told them the man and the woman ... not the Indian had been spotted and could be heading their way. The patrol cars had lost them for the moment.

'Get down to the lobby, Max,' Lepski said when Beigler had switched off. 'This could be action.'

As Jacoby left the office, Lepski alerted the other four detectives over the radio.

But it wasn't until 12.15 that the long wait was rewarded.

Jacoby spotted her first, then as she walked purposely across to the line of telephone booths, Lepski saw her.

He stared searchingly at her: a tall girl with blonde lank hair, dirty, with a sullen face and a tallow complexion. As he watched her push open the door to Booth B he was certain this was the woman they were waiting for.

He flicked down the switch of his radio.

'Looks like she's arrived! She's blonde, white sweater and blue hipsters. She's in the booth now. Don't crowd her ... tail her from a distance!' He switched off.

Leaving the office, he went quickly down the stairs and into the lobby.

127

The girl was walking away, swinging her handbag. Jacoby was starting after her.

Lepski darted to the telephone booth as a large, fat man was opening the door.

'Police!' Lepski snarled in his cop voice, shouldered the man out of his way and felt under the coin box. The envelope was gone! He side stepped the fat man who was goggling at him then walked swiftly after Jacoby.

This was the woman!

He switched on his two-way radio.

'This is it! She's coming out now!' He paused in the sunlight as the girl made her way towards the parking lot. He nodded his approval as he saw Jacoby turn aside and make for his car. 'She's crossing to the car park Dave! Take your car to the North exit and wait. Buick 55789. Pick them up if they come your way. Andy! Cover the south exit!' Switching off, he ran to Jacoby's car and scrambled in. Jacoby had the radio going and he was filling the air with instructions to the six patrol cars circling within a mile of the airport.

The drivers of the patrol cars knew what to do. Each car fanned out to cover every exit from the City. That was their job. The three police cars at the airport would cover the Buick if it headed back to the City.

Dave Farrell came on the air.

'Exit north, Tom and heading out of town. Am covering.'

'Let's go,' Lepski said, and Jacoby set the car moving.

*

David Jackson junior had gone to bed drunk and woken up drunk. This morning at the airport he had to meet his mother who was flying down from New York on a visit. He was fond of his mother, but he wished to hell she hadn't decided to come to Paradise City at this time when he was having a ball at the Spanish hotel. But his mother was important to him. She was his life line, and there were times when he appreciated her. He knew she was the oil in the cogs between his father and himself. If it wasn't for her firm and constant intervention, David Jackson junior would have been disinherited long ago and since his father was worth some fifteen million dollars, the thought of being disinherited fazzed David Jackson junior more than somewhat as the late Damon Runyon would have put it.

So when he came awake, he dragged himself out of his bed knowing the least he could do was to be at the airport on time to meet the old girl even if it killed him. He had a hangover that made him feel as if he had been fed through a mincer. As he got into his E type Jag, to ease his raging headache, he took a long slug from the bottle of Teachers he always kept in his car.

He looked at his gold Omega and saw he had only fifteen minutes to reach the airport before his mother's plane arrived.

With his back teeth practically floating in Scotch, this seemed to him to be a challenge, and he went storming down the boulevard, heading for the airport with the speed of a Grand Prix race and the skill of an idiot child.

He avoided three collisions only because of the other drivers' skill. Then he was out of the traffic and onto the highway and he trod down on the gas pedal. The car surged forward. He looked at his watch. The time was 12.30. When driving at 110 miles an hour it is unwise to take your eye off the road and fatal to look at your watch.

The long hood of the Jag smashed into the side of a dusty blue Buick as the Buick swung out onto the highway from the road leading from the airport.

The force of the impact threw the Buick across the highway and another car, unable to stop, smashed into it, collapsing the radiator.

The Jag left the road, somersaulted and landed on its back, then burst into flames. David Jackson junior had died before the flames began to turn his body into a charred lump of meat.

Chuck saw the Jaguar coming at him, but there was nothing he could do about it. He felt the shock of the impact and then window glass sprayed him like shrapnel.

By some odd freak the car doors flew off and came away from the body of the car. Also by some odd freak, Chuck was thrown from the car to land on hands and knees on the road.

He remained like that staring with terror at the growing pool of blood that made a puddle around him, knowing it was his blood. And yet even with the pain, the terror and the fact he knew he was bleeding to death, all he could think about was the money in the glove compartment of the Buick. Somehow he struggled to his feet. Dimly, he heard cars hooting and voices shouting. Not caring, he lurched to the ruined Buick and reached for the money.

A river of burning gasoline from the Jaguar came like an

orange and red snake down the slope of the road and reached the
Buick as Chuck's bleeding fingers closed on the envelope in
the glove compartment.

The leaking gas tank of the Buick exploded.

Chuck was tossed in the air, his clothes alight, and what was
left of him smashed down across the upended wheels of the
Jaguar.

Eight

As the third car in the collision erupted into flames, as Lepski
and Jacoby fought their way through the gaping crowd, as
black smoke blotted out Chuck's dead body, a brown hand
closed around Meg's wrist and pulled her away from the flames
and the smoke.

Meg was in shock.

She had escaped the flying glass, but the impact of the collision had been so violent it seemed to her that her brain had
come loose inside her head. She felt herself being drawn along
and she was just able to keep walking. She was sightless and
trembling, feeling herself brushing against bodies as the Indian
dragged her through the crowd. People stared at her before
looking back at the burning cars.

When the gas tank of the third car exploded, the crowd
heaved back and Meg dropped to her knees. She felt herself
dragged upright, felt firm, hard hands take hold of her, then
she fainted.

The Indian who had hold of her, stooped and catching hold
of the back of her thighs, he got her over his shoulder. He
started forward, his head down, forcing his way through the
crowd, his movements hidden by the black smoke, billowing
from the burning cars.

Those who noticed him imagined he was rescuing some
dumb girl who had sparked out. The smell of roasting bodies,
the fierce flames and the thick smoke were far more exciting than

to bother with some Indian carrying away a dirty, hippy girl. The crowd let him through, then surged forward as Chuck's body began to burn.

Dave Farrell from his police car, watching all this from the North exit of the airport, alerted Beigler.

'We have a major smash here,' he reported. 'Highway completely blocked. We want help. Buick 55789 involved. Airport fire squad in action. Major traffic snarl up. Repeat ... we want help.'

By this time Lepski, followed by Jacoby, had fought his way through the crowd and the smoke to the burning Buick. The two detectives saw the flames licking around Chuck's body as it lay across the rear wheels of the upturned Jaguar. The heat was so fierce they couldn't get within yards of the burning body.

With sirens screaming, the Airport fire squad arrived and began to blanket the three blazing cars with foam.

It was some ten minutes later before Lepski could report to Beigler. After listening to his report, Beigler told him to come back to headquarters and leave the other detectives to help unscramble the traffic snarl up.

The Indian who had pulled Meg from the wrecked Buick sat in the high cabin of his fifteen ton truck, his hands resting on the steering wheel while he waited patiently for the police to sort out the traffic jam and he could move off.

Meg lay huddled out of sight on the floor of the cab. She was still unconscious and the Indian whose name was Manatee looked doubtfully at her.

Manatee was a slim, narrow-eyed Indian with a crop of black hair that resembled a nylon broom. He was twenty-seven years of age, married with four children. He made a decent living by driving one of Ocida's trucks, carrying crates of oranges to the airport from the market. Manatee had served three years in a tough State prison farm for robbery with violence. If it hadn't been for Ocida who knew the right strings to pull, Manatee wouldn't have got a licence as a truck driver and he and his family would probably have starved. Manatee was very aware of the debt he owed Ocida and was accordingly grateful. There were no secrets kept among the waterfront Indians : most of them knew that Poke Toholo had found a paying racket and he was terrorising the rich whites of the Fifty Club. This was something most of them would liked to have done given the brains, the idea and the nerve. The fact that Poke was in with Ocida and a friend of Jupiter Lucie from whom Manatee got his oranges, made him Manatee's friend also.

Manatee recognised Poke's Buick as Chuck drove away from the airport. He had heard that Poke was working with two whites and he guessed the driver and the girl at his side were these two he had heard about.

When the smash came, Manatee's truck was standing in a parking bay. He had finished unloading two hundred crates of oranges and he was taking time off to smoke a cigarette and rest a little. He was horrified to see Poke's car turn into flames. He saw the girl fall out of the car and he had acted, swiftly and instinctively.

Now, here she was, lying at his feet. Her face pinched and bloodless and her eyes closed.

Manatee began to wonder if he had done the right thing. Maybe he shouldn't have interfered. Maybe she was badly hurt. Maybe she should be in hospital.

He put his hand on her shoulder and gently shook her. Meg's eyes opened. She stared dazedly up at him. For a moment she thought the man leaning over her was Poke, then she realised this was a stranger. She also realised she was half lying on the floor of the cab and she struggled to sit up. Then she remembered the smash and seeing Chuck for a brief, awful moment falling out of the car with his face full of glass.

'Are you all right, lady?' Manatee asked. 'Are you hurt?'

Was she hurt? She moved but felt no pain.

'I'm all right. What happened to . . . him?'

'I guess he got burned.'

Meg shuddered, then she relaxed back against the dirty seat of the cab. She was free, she told herself, she could begin again. She could . . . then she began to shake and she put her head in her hands as the shock hit her.

Manatee saw the traffic was moving again. This delay was costing him money. He started the engine.

'You want me to take you to hospital?' he asked, troubled by the way she was shaking.

'No.'

'I picked up your handbag. lady. You dropped it when you passed out. It's right there by you.'

Meg tried to control her shivering.

'You take it easy. I'll drop you off on the waterfront. Will that be okay?'

'Yes . . . thank you.'

The truck edged into the stream of traffic waved on by a red faced, sweating patrolman.

*

'We had them covered, then this goddamn Jag came like a bat out of hell and soured the whole operation,' Lepski was saying.

Terrell listened. Sitting on the window sill, Beigler also listened.

'Okay. The man's dead, but where's the girl?' Terrell asked.

'She was in the car. I saw her get in,' Lepski said. 'Then came the smash. The smoke as dense and the snarl up something. We had something like five hundred people milling around. Somehow she must have slipped away.' Lepski was aware he had to excuse himself and he was leaning over backwards to do just that.

'So we're back to square A,' Beigler said, his voice flat and resigned.

Terrell stared at his pipe while he thought, then he lifted his heavy shoulders.

'Yes. I'll now have to talk to Hedley We'll have to do it the hard way. I'll see if Hedley will offer a reward. We'll have to give out we want to talk to Poke Toholo. We'll have to set up road blocks and take the Indian quarter to pieces to find him.'

A tap came on the door and Jack Hatchee from the Records department came in.

Hatchee was a tall, heavily built Indian with greying hair, a droopy thick moustache and shrewd black eyes of a thinker. He was a man the detectives at headquarters had learned to respect. If they gave him a name, a description, a method of operation, he would nod and sooner or later – Hatchee never hurried – he would come up with a constructive answer.

Under the impact of the recent events, Terrell had forgotten about him, but when he saw him, he suddenly relaxed the way a man will relax when his competent doctor arrives.

'What is it, Jack?'

'I've checked through all those reports, Chief,' Hatchee said. 'I'm sorry to have been so long but there were a lot of them. One report is out of line. Jupiter Lucie hasn't a cousin.'

'Who is Jupiter Lucie?'

'An Indian. He has a good business, exporting oranges and

running a stall on the waterfront,' Hatchee explained. 'He is one of the big men on the waterfront ... a careful, cunning man. He does many illegal deals but he keeps out of trouble. When Lawson and Dodge went to his stall, while checking on the Indians on the waterfront, Lucie was with another man. This man, Lucie told them, was his cousin, Joe Lucie. Lucie has brothers and sisters, but no cousins.'

Listening to this, Lepski suddenly remembered what his wife had told him: what the old rum-dum Mehitabel Bessinger had told her: *You should look for this man among oranges.*

The old crystal ball gazer had already said the man they had to look for was an Indian and she had been right! Now ... !

He leaned forward, staring at Hatchee.

'This guy deals in oranges?'

The strangled note in his voice made both Terrell and Beigler look at him.

'He has a very good trade in oranges.'

Lepski drew in a snorting breath.

'That's him! I ...' Then he stopped short. The thought of telling Terrell and Beigler that his wife had consulted a crystal ball gazer and the reaction he would get from them brought him out in a hot sweat.

'Something on your mind, Tom?' Beigler asked impatiently.

'I've got a hunch.' Lepski shifted around on his chair with embarrassment. 'I ...'

Terrell and Beigler turned their attention back to Hatchee. Hunches didn't interest them: they wanted facts.

'So okay, Lucie hasn't a cousin ... we'll check him out,' Terrell turned to Lepski. 'Go down to Lucie's stall and talk to this guy who Lucie says is his cousin.'

Lepski was now certain that this man he was being told to talk to was Poke Toholo. That old rum-dum might be swilling his whisky, but she had delivered the goods once and he was now sure she was delivering the goods again.

'Chief ... suppose this man is Toholo.' he said, sitting forward as he looked directly at Terrell. 'So I check him out. So where does it get me? I don't know Toholo. I've never seen him. None of us have seen him. I could be walking into a bullet. Okay, maybe this guy is some punk out of jail who Lucie is taking care of, but if he is Toholo, I could walk into trouble and bitch up the whole operation.'

'He's right,' Hatchee said quietly. 'If it is Toholo there will be trouble.'

Terrell nodded. By his sudden frown the three detectives knew he was annoyed with himself for not thinking of this possibility.

'Yes.'

Terrell thought for a long moment, then he reached for the telephone.

'Charlie ... see if you can get me Mr. Rodney Branzenstein. Yeah ... Branzenstein. Try the Fifty Club.'

After a brief wait, Branzenstein came on the line.

'Rod ... can I ask you a favour? Will you do a little police work for me?' Terrell asked.

'Well, for God's sake!' Branzenstein laughed. 'Police work! What do you mean?'

Terrell explained.

'Well, of course.' Branzenstein's voice turned serious. 'Yes, I would know Poke Toholo anywhere. So what do you want me to do?'

'I'll send a man over to you right away,' Terrell said. 'He'll point out Lucie's stall. I want you to walk past and see if you spot Toholo. Be careful. Don't let him think you've recognised him.'

'I understand. This will be an outing for me! Okay, Frank, send your man down. I'll be waiting.'

'He'll do it,' Terrell said as he hung up. 'Jack, go to the Fifty Club and take Branzenstein to the waterfront. Show him Lucie's stall, but keep out of sight yourself. I don't have to tell you what to do.' He turned to Lepski. 'Go with him and cover Branzenstein. By the time you get there, I'll have the whole waterfront sealed off. Get moving!'

When Lepski and Hatchee had gone, Terrell looked at Beigler.

'This could be a tricky one ... the waterfront is always crowded. If it is Toholo, he could make a fight of it. We know he has a gun.' He opened a desk drawer, searched and brought out a large scale map of the waterfront. He studied it for a minute or so, then began to mark the map with a pencil. 'Cover all these streets I've marked, Joe. If it is Toholo, we get him dead or alive.'

Beigler nodded and taking the map, he went back to his

desk. Picking up the microphone, he began alerting his men, bringing them fast in a wide semi-circle that would surround and seal off the waterfront.

*

Rodney Branzenstein got out of the police car, followed by Lepski and Jack Hatchee.

'All right, you fellows,' Branzenstein said, very much in control of the operation, 'just show me where you think this Indian is and leave it to me. I know just what your Chief wants. If it is Toholo, I'll take out my handkerchief and make as if I'm mopping my brow.'

Lepski had many hates: among them were rich Corporation lawyers who owned Rolls-Royces and lived in ten bedroom houses.

To Lepski, Branzenstein was like a matador's cape to a bull.

'Mop your . . . what?' Lepski asked.

Branzenstein regarded the lean detective and recognised the hostility in the hard, blue eyes.

'Brow . . . forehead . . . the top part of my face,' Branzenstein said sarcastically. 'Like this.' He took out an immaculately white handkerchief and passed it over his forehead. 'Are you with me?'

Lepski hated him even more.

'Yeah.' He turned to Hatchee who was watching this scene with amusement but with a wooden face. 'I'll go ahead, Jack. The nineteenth stall on the right?'

'That's it.'

Lepski walked away, mingling with the crowd. He began to count the stalls. At the nineteenth there was a white man talking to a fat Indian and nearby a young Indian. Lepski looked searchingly at the young Indian as he passed, imprinting his features and the way he was dressed on his police trained mind. This could be Poke Toholo, but he would have to wait until Branzenstein identified him.

After giving Lepski time to get clear, Hatchee led Branzenstein along the waterfront. After they had weaved their way through the crowd for some hundred yards, Hatchee stopped.

'The stall is right ahead, sir,' he said. 'You see that bollard? The stall is opposite.'

Branzenstein stared at the bollard, then nodded. He was suddenly assailed with doubts. He began asking himself what he was doing out here in the burning heat working for the police. Goddamn it! After all he was one of the most successful ... what was he thinking? ... *the* most successful Corporation lawyer in the City and somehow he had been persuaded into trying to identify a lunatic Indian! He could be walking to his death!

Seeing Branzenstein suddenly lose colour and was hesitating, Hatchee, who knew the signs of fear, said quietly, 'That bollard just ahead, sir.'

Branzenstein found he had come out in a cold sweat.

'Yes ... yes ... I'm not blind!'

'Okay, sir. Lepski will be covering you. Lepski is the best shot on the force, sir.'

Hatchee hoped t'iis white man might be comforted to know he was being protected, but it worked the other way. The very idea he was being protected increased Branzenstein's fears.

So they thought there could be shooting! Good God! Branzenstein was on the point of calling off the operation when he saw this elderly Indian was regarding him, his black eyes calm, but probing.

He pulled himself together. He couldn't let this Indian know how frightened he was.

'Fine,' he said huskily. 'I'll get going,' and he started towards the distant bollard.

He had to force his way through the crowd. The noise, the shouts of the vendors and the raucous voices of the tourists heightened his tension. He reached the bollard.

Opposite the bollard was a line of fruit stalls. His heart thumping, Branzenstein paused. He was suddenly too frightened to look at the stalls. Instead, he turned and stared across the oily water of the harbour.

Watching him, Lepski groaned. Could this fat slob be chickening out? he asked himself.

Lepski was standing in the shadow of an archway that led to the better fish restaurants along the waterfront. The smell of frying fish made him hungry. He realised he hadn't eaten a decent meal in the past fifty hours.

He forced his attention back to Branzenstein. What was the matter with the creep? He was acting like a television subject on the screen for the first time.

He watched Branzenstein turn and look at the fruit stalls. He saw him stiffen, stare, then take out his handkerchief and wipe his forehead.

137

It was the corniest performance Lepski had ever seen: so corny it attracted the attention of the tourists who reacted as a crowd will react when someone stares up at an empty sky: almost instantly there are hundreds of upturned faces.

Lepski cursed under his breath.

Poke Toholo was leaning against a crate of oranges. Jupiter Lucie was making a bargain with the fruit buyer of the Spanish hotel to supply the hotel with eight crates of oranges a day. Their bargaining had become bitter. This wasn't Poke's business. He kept looking at his cheap wrist watch. By now Chuck must have collected all the envelopes.

But could Chuck be trusted?

Five envelopes . . . two thousand five hundred dollars!

Poke picked up an orange and squeezed it as he thought.

It had been a good idea, but the colour of his skin had forced him to use Chuck and the girl. He knew once he used them, the money was automatically in danger.

He recalled the moment when he had been waiting for Chuck to bring him the money and when Chuck had come into the room. The sudden expression of fear and shock on Chuck's face when he had stood in the doorway had warned Poke that Chuck could betray him.

How easy it would be for Chuck to drive away in the car with this next lot of money.

Poke felt the juice of the orange running down his wrist and he realised he had squeezed the orange flat while his thoughts tormented him. He dropped what was left of the fruit and wiped his hand on the seat of his jeans.

Lucie and the fruit buyer had completed their deal. They were now smiling and shaking hands.

Poke looked across the crowded quay at the oily water of the harbour. The oil on the water made a rainbow of floating colours. Then he saw Branzenstein.

Poke immediately recognised the fat, handsome man. When Poke had worked as a barman at the Fifty Club he had had to endure this man's arrogance and his patronising tolerance for Indians. Branzenstein had always been polite to him and Poke had resented this more than the way the other members of the Club had treated him. He had listened to Branzenstein sounding off to the other members that 'After all, non-whites are human.'

Poke remembered Branzenstein talking in a loud voice to Jefferson Lacey who despised coloured people.

You have to admit they are hard working and industrious. Can you imagine how this club could survive without them? I like them. They're nice people. What's that? Look, Jeff, that is a stupid argument if I may say so. Make them members of this Club? We wouldn't want Negroes here either, now would we?

With smouldering hatred, Poke watched Branzenstein's uneasy antics.

The Toholo family were Catholics. Before Poke left home, he always went with his father to Sunday Mass.

Kneeling in the dimly lit church with its awe inspiring, flickering candles, Poke watched his father, kneeling at his side, through his laced fingers as he pretended to pray. The peace on the old man's face as he looked towards the altar filled Poke with despair. This was a peace he would never know.

He recalled a sentence a priest had used when delivering an uninspired, hurriedly delivered address.

And then came the kiss of Judas: the time accepted gesture of betrayal.

Poke watched Branzenstein look directly at him and he knew Branzenstein had recognised him. He watched him take out his handkerchief and wipe it across his face and he knew Branzenstein was betraying him.

The crooked cell in Poke's brain sparked like the white flare of an exploding flashlight bulb.

He looked quickly to right and left as a wild animal will look when it senses danger. He knew instinctively that somewhere out of sight, the police were waiting for this signal.

Jupiter Lucie was busy writing in his order book. The fruit buyer, satisfied with his bargain, was walking away.

Lepski saw Branzenstein flourish his handkerchief. So this Indian was Toholo! He switched on his radio.

As he did so, Poke slid his hand under the shelf of the stall and his brown fingers closed around the butt of the .38 automatic. His thin lips came off his teeth in a savage snarl.

Glancing up, Lucie saw the mad, murderous expression on Poke's face and he dropped his notebook and cringed away.

Lepski was saying into the microphones: 'Branzenstein has identified Toholo. Over for action.'

Branzenstein had done what Terrell had asked him to do. He

139

began to walk away. He was shaking a little and still frightened. This was now up to the police, he told himself. This was something he would never do again. But as he kept walking, moving through the crowd, he suddenly realised he would be able to dine out on this story for weeks. He began to imagine how his friends would react as he recounted how he had helped trap the Executioner.

It was at this moment as he was beginning to relax and preen himself at the thought of impressing his friends when a .38 bullet smashed into the back of his head.

*

Listening to Terrell's instructions, Lepski had taken his eyes off Branzenstein for a brief moment. He heard the shot, looked in time to see Branzenstein fall and his eyes shifted to where Toholo had been, but the Indian was no longer there.

Lepski was caught in two minds. Should he report what had happened or go after Toholo?

In this brief second of hesitation, the Indians, working at the fruit stalls and who had seen what had happened, made enough confusion to allow Poke to slip away.

In another second the waterfront erupted into panic, screams and jostling Indians, apparently terrified, who ran to and fro, creating more panic.

Lepski saw it was hopeless to go after Toholo even if he knew which way he had gone. The heaving barrier of people between him and Lucie's stall was now impassable. Two Indians, pretending panic, overturned a rival's fruit stall and oranges began to roll in waves around Lepski's feet.

He switched on his radio and reported what had happened.

Back at headquarters, Terrell and Beigler listened to Lepski's commentary.

The two men stared at each other.

Beigler had never see his Chief fazzed and now looking at Terrell's sudden white face and shocked eyes, Beigler realised this big, solid man could be fazzed.

'The waterfront is sealed off, Joe?' Terrell asked as he got to his feet.

Beigler stood up.

'It's sealed off.'

'Then we go in and flush him out,' Terrell said. He pulled

open a drawer in his desk and took out a .38 police special and harness. He took off his coat and slid on the harness.

'Look Chief,' Beigler said uneasily, 'I'll go. Someone has to stay here. There'll be calls coming in . . . and . . .'

Terrell stared at him.

'I'm handling this field operation,' he said quietly. 'You stay here. I sent a friend of mine to his death. This is a personal thing,' and he left the office.

Beigler hesitated, then contacted Lepski on the radio.

'The Chief's coming down, Tom,' he said. 'He imagines he's responsible for Branzenstein's death. In the mood he's in, he could walk into a bullet. You get it?'

'I've got it,' Lepski said and switched off.

*

Poke felt a surge of vicious satisfaction run through him when he saw Branzenstein fall. This was the moment to go into hiding. Even as he was pulling the trigger, he decided what the next immediate move was to be.

As Branzenstein dropped, Poke ducked low, shoved Jupiter Lucie out of his way and darted into a small junk shop not four yards from the fruit stall.

This junk shop was run by an eighty-year-old Indian who sold everything from bows and arrows, strings of beads to alligator skins. He was one of Ocida's contact men. It had been Ocida's money that had financed the junk in the shop. He was one of the many pairs of eyes that kept Ocida informed about what was going on on the waterfront.

This old Indian's name was Micco. He was sitting in the doorway of his tiny shop, stringing glass beads onto a thread when the shooting occurred.

As Poke darted past him into the darkness of the shop, Micco pushed his long needle into the box full of beads, collecting eight more beads to go in the thread.

He knew in a few minutes the waterfront would be swarming with police. He had seen the shooting. This had been a stupid, bad act, but it had been done by an Indian. He knew about Poke and his racket. When he had first heard about it it had amused him and he had nodded his approval, but now Poke was showing how sick he was and this began to worry Micco, but Poke was still an Indian.

Micco was a close friend of Poke's father. Micco pitied the old man because he was too honest. He knew how the old man would suffer when he heard what had happened. Sooner or later, Poke would be caught. This was inevitable. Still, Indians had to protect each other. When the police finally came to his shop, as he knew they would, he would stare up at them and put on his idiot's face and pretend to be deaf. After all he was eighty years old. Indians of that age were expected to be idiots and deaf.

As Poke went swiftly to the back of the shop and opened a door that led to the upper storey he was feeling very confident.

The waterfront was a warren of escape routes. There were roofs, cellars, tiny, smelly rooms, steep, dark stairs, more tiny rooms, other roofs, alleys, brick walls into other alleys, fire escapes to more roofs and then to lower roofs, skylights into passages lined by doors that hid cupboard-like rooms where the Indians lived when not making a living on the waterfront.

Poke knew all this. Some months ago, an instinctive feeling to survive had urged him to reconnoitre the whole of the waterfront. He had set about the task as a man will plan a long, complicated journey with maps, figuring mileages, deciding whether to take this road or that road.

The Indians never asked questions. Some of them were puzzled by the way Poke investigated their lodging houses, by the way he climbed to their roofs, by the way he ran along the smelly alleys, but it wasn't their business ... maybe the boy was crazy. They had a living to make ... so why bother?

Now Poke realised this past urge to survive was paying off.

He was sure the police knew he was the Executioner. Somehow they had discovered he was working with Jupiter Lucie. Before they could come after him, they had to identify him. So Branzenstein was the one they had asked to betray him.

As he climbed through the skylight onto the roof, he was glad that he had killed yet another of the rich slobs belonging to the Fifty Club.

For a long moment he paused in the hot sunshine, trying to think clearly. His mind reacted like the mind of a man lost in a labyrinth: not sure whether to turn right or left or go straight ahead.

Then he decided he must go to Ocida. Chuck would be there now with the money. Then he would leave the City. He would have over two thousand five hundred dollars! With a thousand

142

dollars he would be able to bribe the head barman at the Panama Hotel in Miami to give him a job as second barman. A job like that was worth in tips alone two hundred dollars a week! The barman had promised him the job if he gave him a thousand dollars.

It didn't occur to Poke that every policeman in Florida would now be hunting for him. He imagined that once he got away from Paradise City he would be safe.

Cautiously he moved to the edge of the roof and looked down at the teaming waterfront. The scene below was like an overturned ant hill. Women were screaming. People were jostling each other. An ambulance, its siren moaning, had arrived. Policemen, sweating and cursing, were trying to control the crowd. Hundreds of oranges, on which people stepped and slipped, made a carpet around Branzenstein's dead body.

Out of this confusion, Poke saw and recognised Jack Hatchee and he immediately knew this man was deadly dangerous to him. This Cop was an Indian. He knew the waterfront as well as Poke did.

For a brief moment Poke hesitated, then the cell in his brain again exploded like a flashlight bulb.

Resting the gun barrel on his arm, sighting for Hatchee's head, he squeezed the trigger.

*

'You take care of this mess, Jack,' Lepski was saying. 'I'll . . .' That was as far as he got.

He saw Hatchee stagger and a line of blood appear on the side of his greying hair. Then as the big man fell, Lepski heard the shot.

Whirling around, he saw a movement on the roof of one of the many tiny shops that lined the waterfront. His hand flashed to his gun. He drew and fired in a single flowing movement.

Then Andy Shields came through the crowd and reached him.

'He's up there!' Lepski said. 'Come on!'

Dave Farrell barged his way through the crowd and Lepski waved to Hatchee who was stirring.

'Take care of him, Dave,' he said and followed by Shields, he started towards Micco's junk shop. He hadn't taken more than ten steps, fighting his way through the milling crowd when he trod on an orange and took a fall that shook the breath out of him. Shields, trying to break Lepski's fall, skidded on another orange and came down flat on Lepski as Lepski, cursing, was struggling to his feet.

Lepski's shot had been close.

The bullet whistled by Poke's head and chipped cement from a chimney stack spraying splinters back at Poke as he ducked away. A cement splinter caught him under his left eye and he began to bleed.

Keeping low he ran across the roof, holding his handkerchief to his bleeding face. He scrambled down an iron fire escape, paused for a moment as he arrived in a narrow, evil smelling alley, got his bearings, then ran to the right. With the movement of a cat, he slid over a brick wall, landed in another alley, again checked his bearings, then ran left. At the end of the alley was an open doorway. Still holding the blood-stained handkerchief to his face, he went through the doorway and ran up narrow, steep stairs. At the head of the stairs an Indian girl child was playing with a doll on the landing. Poke paused and looked at her, then went on past her. The gun in his hand and the blood-stained handkerchief struck her silent with terror.

At the far end of the passage, Poke found a door. He opened it and again emerged into sunlight. Ducking low, he ran across the flat roof, paused to drag open a skylight, slid down into darkness, leaving bloody finger prints on the skylight frame.

Moving silently, he ran down the steep, narrow stairs, through a door leading to yet another alley. He climbed a wall and dropped into a yard where an enormously fat Indian woman was sitting on a box, plucking a chicken. For a brief moment they stared at each other, then the woman lowered her eyes and continued to pluck the chicken as Poke moved past her and into the shack she called her home.

From there he reached another alley, climbed another wall and finally arrived at the back door of Ocida's rooming house.

By now the cut on his face had ceased to bleed and he stuffed the blood-stained handkerchief into his pocket. He paused in the passage, listening, then moved forward and gently opened a door he knew led into Ocida's sitting-room.

Ocida was sitting in a broken down armchair, his hands resting on his fat knees. He was talking to Manatee who had just arrived.

It took a moment, in semi-darkness, for Poke to recognise

Manatee. With a quick, sly movement, Poke slid his gun into the back pocket of his hipsters. He moved into the room and closed the door.

Ocida leaned back in his chair. His fat face unsmiling, his eyes shifty.

'This has become bad for you, Poke,' he said. 'Manatee will tell you.'

Briefly, Manatee told Poke what had happened at the airport. Poke listened, his eyes glittering.

'The white man is dead?'

Manatee nodded.

'The car?'

'Finished.'

'And the girl?'

'I brought her as far as the waterfront. She walked away.'

Poke stood thinking. Had the money gone up in flames with the car? Had the girl got it? A vicious spurt of rage ran through him.

He jerked his thumb towards the door.

'Get out!'

Manatee looked at Ocida who nodded. He went quickly from the room.

There was a long pause, then Ocida said quietly, 'You must go away, Poke. I'm sorry it has ended like this. It was a good idea. The accident was bad luck.'

Poke stared at the fat Indian, then he said, 'I need money. I need a thousand dollars.'

Ocida flinched. Looking at Poke, seeing the expression on his face and the glitter in his eyes, he realised he was in a dangerous situation.

He thought of the gun he always kept in the top drawer of his desk. The desk stood four yards from where he was sitting. The gun was a .45 Colt automatic which he had bought from an Army sergeant and which he never believed he would use. He had taken pride in the gun. Every so often he cleaned and oiled it. Now, looking at Poke's face, he realised this gun ... if he could reach it ... could save his life for he was suddenly certain his life was in danger. But sitting in this broken down armchair, he knew he couldn't reach the gun before Poke killed him. He must, he told himself, use a little bluff.

'If I had so much money, you would have it,' he said. 'Your

father and I are good friends. It would be my pleasure to give it to you.'

'Never mind about my father ... give me the money,' Poke said and his hand went behind him and reappeared, holding his gun.

Ocida nodded. He got slowly to his feet and walked over to the desk. As he reached to pull open the top drawer where the gun was, his big body shielding his movement, he felt Poke's gun dig into his back and he knew he was defeated. His hand moved from the top drawer to the second drawer which he opened. It was in this drawer that he kept his cash.

'There ... that is all I have,' he said. 'Help yourself.'

Poke shoved him aside and snatched up a thick packet of dollar bills. He thrust the bills into his shirt and moved quickly to the door.

Ocida, still sensing danger, stood motionless.

'Remember, Poke, your father and I are good friends,' he said, a quaver in his voice.

'Open the top drawer,' Poke said. 'Go on ... open it!'

They looked at each other for a long moment and Ocida saw the madness in Poke's eyes. Slowly, his heart beginning to hammer, Ocida opened the drawer.

Poke saw the gun lying on a sheet of oil stained blotting paper.

'Good friends?' Poke said and squeezed the trigger of his gun.

The bang of the gun echoed through the building and out onto the waterfront.

As Ocida fell, Poke stepped to the desk, snatched up the .45 Colt, dropped his own gun which was now empty and ran out of the room.

Hearing the shot Detective Alec Horn who was covering this section of the waterfront arrived at the end of the alley leading to Ocida's back entrance as Poke came through the doorway.

For a fraction of a second, Horn hesitated, not sure if this Indian was Poke Toholo. Then seeing the gun in Poke's hand, his own gun flashed up.

Poke was just that fraction of a second ahead of him. Poke's bullet smashed Horn's shoulder and dropped him.

Horn's bullet cut a groove in Poke's left arm.

Poke swung around and ran blindly down the alley. The pain in his arm threw him off balance. For the first time, he felt he was hunted and panic seized him. He reached a door of a two-storey, ramshackled house at the end of the alley, kicked it open and blundered into a dark passage. His one thought now was to hide. Stairs faced him. He raced up them two at the time, reached a landing, then paused. To his right was a lone door and there was no skylight. He realised he had run into a trap.

Then the door swung open and he lifted his gun.

An Indian girl, tall, thin, her skin pock marked, her hair in a plait, coiled around her head, came out on the landing.

She froze at the sight of him.

Poke covered her with his gun.

They stared at each other. Blood was dripping from Poke's fingers, making a puddle on the floor.

'Fix this!' He tapped his wounded arm and again threatened her with the gun.

Her eyes opened very wide and she nodded. She moved back into the room, beckoning to him.

*

When Poke had told Manatee to get out, he had only gone as far as Ocida's store room because he feared for his boss. When he heard the shot, he knew his fear had been realised. He had watched Poke come down the passage, then he had darted into the living-room and had seen the vast body lying on the floor. He had shuddered with horror, then turned and had run down the passage to the back door. He heard the two shots as Poke and Horn had fired at each other.

Cautiously, he peered into the alley. He was in time to see Poke running away, pause, then enter the last house at the end of the alley.

Manatee then saw the wounded detective, struggling to sit up.

If Poke hadn't killed Ocida, Manatee would never have considered for a moment betraying him, but by killing Ocida, Poke had severed the cord that linked him to the fraternity of Indian protection.

Manatee went to the fallen detective as Lepski and Andy Shields swung themselves over the wall.

Lepski's hand dropped on Shields' gun, pushing it down.

'It's not him!' He shoved Manatee aside and knelt by Horn who was now sitting up and grimacing with pain. 'Are you hurt bad?'

Horn shook his head.

147

'He went down there.'

Lepski looked along the filthy cul-de-sac.

'Take care of him, Andy. Radio for help! He must have gone over the wall.'

'Sir!' Manatee was standing now with his back pressed against the wall of the alley. 'He is in the last house at the end of the alley. There's no way out except the way he went in. I know the house. Manee, Ocida's granddaughter, lives there.'

Lepski stared at the Indian, wondering if he could trust him. He knew all the Indians along the waterfront were loyal to each other. This could be a trick to give Poke time to get away.

'He killed my boss, sir,' Manatee said as if knowing how Lepski was thinking. 'He's crazy. He must now be caught. He is in there!'

'You're sure there's no other way out?'

Manatee nodded.

Two police officers came over the wall.

'You two take care of Alec,' Lepski said to them. 'Come on, Andy, let's get him!'

Guns in hand, the two detectives ran down the alley, paused at the open door of the house, then Lepski moved in while Shields covered him.

Lepski saw blood stains on the floor and he looked up the narrow stairs.

He moved back and switched on his radio.

Terrell came on the air.

Lepski reported what was happening and pin pointed where he was.

'We have him bottled up, Chief,' Lepski concluded. 'Andy and I are going up there to take him.'

'Can he get away?' Terrell asked.

'No . . . we have him bottled up.'

'Then hold it, Tom, until I get there. I'm taking him.'

Lepski grimaced. He remembered what Beigler had said about keeping Terrell out of this mess.

'Okay, Chief,' and he switched off. He hesitated for a long moment, then he looked at Shields, 'Let's go get this sonofabitch,' and moving silently, he started up the stairs.

The Indian girl, Manee, finished bandaging Poke's arm. While she worked, he sat on the bed, looking around the tiny, hot room. The door of the room stood open. Over the head of the bed hung a large crucifix. He looked at it, then his eyes shifted away with a pang of guilt. The crucifix made him think of his father and brought back the memory of when they used to kneel together in the church with its smell of incense, the flickering candle light and the peace on his father's face.

'You are Poke Toholo, the son of my grandfather's great friend,' Manee said as she moved away from him. 'Please go now to my grandfather who will help you get away. He never refuses anyone help.'

'Your grandfather?' He sat upright, his eyes widening. 'Ocida?'

She nodded.

'Of course. Go to him. He will help you.'

A wave of utter despair washed over Poke. For a long time now he had been frightened that there was something wrong with his brain. He had refused to believe he couldn't cure himself by will-power. Now, he realised he was really sick. Why had he killed Ocida? He knew now that if he had only asked Ocida to hide him, Ocida would have done so and he would have been safe.

He sat still, feeling the throbbing pain in his arm, the gun resting on his knee. He knew as he sat there, that this was the end of his life. He knew he was beyond help and beyond redemption.

The tenth stair from the top of the staircase was rotten. Poke had come up the stairs two at the time, missing the tenth stair. Manee knew about the stair and always stepped over it, but Lepski trod on it. The stair gave under his weight with a splintering crash. He had his hand on the bannister rail and by clutching onto the rail he just managed to prevent his foot getting trapped. Cursing softly, he jerked his foot free, then knowing he had given himself away by the noise, he raced up the remaining stairs to find himself on a bare landing with an open door on his right. He waved Shields back and flattened himself against the wall, gun in hand.

Sunlight coming through the window of the room with the open door made an oblong patch of light on the dusty floor.

Shields came up the stairs and crouched on the third stair from the top, his gun covering Lepski.

When the stair broke, the noise made Poke stiffen. His eyes darted towards the landing beyond the open door. He lifted his gun.

Manee saw the hopeless despair on his face and she drew away from him.

With his left hand, Poke took the money he had stolen from Ocida from inside his shirt and dropped it on the bed.

'I'm sorry,' he said, looking at the girl. 'I am very sick. There is something wrong with my head.' He pointed to the money. 'This now belongs to you.' He hesitated, then went on, 'I killed your grandfather. It is his money. I took it. It belongs to you.'

Creeping along the wall, Lepski paused to listen.

Manee looked at the pile of money lying on the dirty white quilt. She had never seen so much money. Her eyes opened wide.

'This is mine?'

Thoughts flashed through her mind. If this money was really for her a door would open into a new life. This room, the smell and the noise of the waterfront, the groping fingers moving up her skirt when she worked in the restaurant, the white sailors she had to bring back here when she wanted new clothes ... all this and more would be wiped away with this money.

'Take it,' Poke said, watching her.

'You really mean it's for me?'

She couldn't believe it as she stared at the money.

'I killed your grandfather,' Poke said and realised she wasn't listening. All she was thinking about was the money. He felt a surge of hatred run through him. 'Take it and get out!'

She snatched up the money and ran out onto the landing.

Lepski caught hold of her wrist and swung her into Shields' arms. Shields clapped his hand over her mouth.

Sitting on the bed, Poke stared through the open doorway. His mind came alive with pictures of past hatreds: the Club, his father's servility, the rich, the arrogant, the unkind and the patronising.

He had often thought of death. The kindest way to die, he had thought, would be to be like a lamp when the wick is turned down. Slowly the light would diminish and finally go out. But now he knew there would be no slow turning down of the wick. As he saw Lepski's shadow come into the oblong of sunlight, he looked at the crucifix on the wall. Staring at the crucifix, suddenly hopeful, he put the gun barrel in his mouth and pulled the trigger.

*

'Are you looking for company?'

Meg stiffened and looked up.

For the past two hours she had been sitting on a stone bench at the far end of the harbour, alone, except for a fish hawk that circled above her.

By now she had absorbed the shock of the crash. Now, she was beginning to wonder what to do. She had no money. Her clothes were at the rooming house and she was sure if she went to collect them, the fat Indian would demand payment for the rent of the room. Besides, Poke might be waiting there. She couldn't go back, so she had nothing but what she had on.

She had lost her gold-plated meal ticket, she thought bitterly. Some meal ticket! She lifted her long hair off her shoulders in a helpless gesture. Well, she thought, she would have to find some other man who would buy her the few things she needed. There was always some man around who would help her so long as she was willing to lie on her back.

Are you looking for company?

The very words Chuck had used when he had picked her up and then this awful mess had started.

She looked at the young man, standing by her side.

What a freak! she thought.

He was tall and painfully thin with a chin beard and he wore glasses. The lenses were so thick they made his eyes look like brown gooseberries. He wore a grey open neck shirt, tucked into black pants and a broad leather belt with a tarnished brass buckle around his tiny waist.

At least, Meg thought, he was clean so he could have some money. It was when they were dirty, as she was, there was no money.

Her mouth moved into a forced smile.

'Hello,' she said. 'Where did you spring from?'

'I saw you. You looked lonely.' He pulled at his beard as if hoping she would notice it. 'Are you lonely?'

His voice was soft and without character. As she studied him, she felt a pang of disappointment. Her hope of *here is someone* wasn't going to be fulfilled by this freak.

Still, in her present position, she couldn't afford to be selective so she said, 'I guess I am.'

'Mind if I join you?'

'I don't mind.'

He came around the stone bench and sat by her side.

151

'I'm Mark Lees. What's your name?'

'Meg.'

'Just ... Meg?'

She nodded.

There was a long pause. She looked up and watched the circling fish hawk. If only she could wave a magic wand and be up there with him. He would be someone. She was sure of that. How marvellous to be able to circle the sea, to dive on a fish, to be utterly free!

'Are you on vacation?'

She frowned, then came back to earth.

'What?'

'Are you on vacation?'

'Are you?'

'No. I lost my job yesterday. I'm trying to make up my mind what to do and where to go.'

She felt a tiny wave of sympathy for him.

'Like me: I'm trying to make up my mind what to do too.'

He looked at her, then away. A swift, shifty look, but she knew it had taken in her full breasts and her long legs. It was so easy, she thought. Men are such stupid animals.

'I'm sick of this City. It's too expensive. It's only for the rich. I have a car.' He again looked at her. 'I thought I'd go to Jacksonville. I've a friend there. He could get me a job.' Again the shifty look at her breasts. 'Do you want to come along with me for the ride?'

She didn't hesitate.

'I don't mind.'

He seemed to relax a little and again he fingered his beard.

'That's fine. Where are your things? I'll get the car and pick you up.'

It was her turn now to study him. His thin face showed no animation. He was staring down at his thin, bony hands, resting on his knees. She felt a moment of hesitation. Maybe he was a sex maniac. She pondered for a few seconds, then she mentally shrugged. It was only if you resisted a sex maniac that he became dangerous. She had to leave Paradise City. Jacksonville was as good as anywhere to go to.

'I haven't anything,' she said. 'No money ... no clothes ... no nothing.'

'You have something ... all girls have.' He got to his feet. 'Let's go.'

They walked together in silence along the harbour wall and to the car park. He led her to a beaten up T.R.4.

As they got into the car, he said without looking at her, 'I want to make sex with you . . . you will, won't you?'

She knew this was coming and she thought of the moment when this dreary freak would take her and her body cringed.

'Have you any money?' she asked.

He looked swiftly at her, then away.

'What's that to do with it?' he asked blankly.

'You'll find out.'

Then she saw her reflection in the windshield and she grimaced.

God! What a mess she looked . . . her hair!

She opened her bag for her comb and she stiffened, her heart skipping a beat. Inside the bag was a brown manilla envelope . . . the envelope she had collected from the airport. The crash had happened so quickly she hadn't had time to put it with the other envelopes in the glove compartment and she had completely forgotten it.

Quickly, she closed the bag.

Five hundred dollars!

The freak at her side was trying to start the car, pressing the starter button and muttering to himself.

She was free! Like the fish hawk! She wouldn't have to have this freak moaning and groaning on top of her!

Five hundred dollars!

She opened the car door and got out.

'Hey!' He stared up at her as she slammed the car door. 'Where are you going?'

'Anywhere but with you,' she said and walked away.

Later, again sitting on the stone bench at the end of the harbour with the fish hawk circling above her, she opened the envelope with trembling, expectant fingers.

The envelope contained no money.

At least one member of the Fifty Club had courage.

Written on the expensive, embossed notepaper of the Club in firm, flowing handwriting was the message:
Go to hell.

www.ingramcontent.com/pod-product-compliance
Ingram Content Group UK Ltd.
Pitfield, Milton Keynes, MK11 3LW, UK
UKHW022308280225
455674UK00004B/222